Family money

How to afford your children

Nigel Smith

Adamson Books
Ely, Cambridgeshire

For Becky and Zoe

Text copyright © 1988 Nigel Smith
Additional research by Lynette Gilbert

Published by Adamson Books
Akeman House, High Street,
Stretham, Ely,
Cambridgeshire CB6 3JQ

Cover design by Simon Bell
Book design by Nicky Adamson

British Library Cataloguing in Publication Data
Smith, Nigel
　　Family money: how to afford your children
　　1. Great Britain. Personal finance – for
　　graduates
　　I. Title
　　332.024'00941

ISBN 0-948543-20-5

All rights reserved. No part of this publication may be reproduced, stored in a retrieval system, or transmitted, in any form or by any means, electronic, mechanical, photocopying, recording or otherwise, without the prior permission of the publishers. Such permission, if granted, is subject to a fee depending on the nature of the use.

Typeset by CRB Typesetting Services, Ely, Cambs
Printed in Great Britain by the Hollen Street Press

Contents

	Introduction	6
1	Before the first baby	11
2	Baby benefits	25
3	State help for families	34
4	Separation and divorce	54
5	Single parents and unmarried couples	70
6	While you are at work	77
7	Children's income and savings	87
8	Safeguarding the family's future	107
9	Education and after	120
10	Leaving money to children	135
11	Further information	150
	Index	158

Introduction

Having children is probably the greatest investment you ever make. You may not have looked at it that way before, but children are an asset into which you will undoubtedly put a lot of cash and from which you will certainly be very well rewarded. Of course there are times when they can be little horrors and when we all wonder if we did the right thing, but there are hopefully many more times when we know without doubt that having them was the best decision we ever made.

But for many families there will be times when they feel the pinch. If one income is having to support four or five people, there are bound to be times when parents feel poor in comparison with childless couples who both work. The money seems to slip away as fast as it can be earned, with not very much to show for it, it seems. But when you add up the total cost of having a child, it is hardly surprising. The figures below show that it might cost an astronomical £51,500 to support a child from birth to school-leaving age – more if you take more than five years off work or if your child goes to an independent school or is partly dependent on you after 16.

The figures are, of course, rough-and-ready but they were fairly typical at the time of writing. Inflation will mean that many of the actual figures turn out to be higher in future, but you can work on the assumption that the costs will be much the same as the current value of the amounts given. And the figures make a number of assumptions, most notably that there are three-year gaps between children and that quite a lot in the way of baby equipment, clothes and so on is passed on from one child to the next; that one parent will give up work until the youngest child goes to school, and that this parent could earn £6,600 a year which, after tax and National Insurance contributions have been deducted, would leave about £5,000; that the other parent earns £8,000 and pays £2,000 mortgage interest a year; and that until the youngest child is 13 it is necessary to employ someone to look after the children both in school holidays and on school days between the end of school and the parents' returning from work.

On these assumptions, the loss of one parent's income would cost £5,000 a year for five years for the first child, making £25,000, and three extra years at £5,000 a year for each subsequent child. Maternity items and baby equipment could well come to £750 for the first child, and, say, £250 for each subsequent one. The 'running costs' of the first child (clothes, food, toys, books, toiletries, etc) might come to £800 a year for sixteen years, with £600 for each subsequent child. From five years to thirteen (with both parents working) the cost of nannies, babysitters, etc, could be some £2,000 a year for those eight years. From five to sixteen years, the average pocket money given to children costs £730 for each child, and the cost of parties, outings, trips and holidays might come to £2,750 for the first child and £2,000 for each subsequent one. That adds up to a total cost of £57,980 for the first child and £27,550 for each subsequent one.

From this you can deduct £563 for maternity benefits for the first child (only), and child benefit at £7.25 a week for each child. This leaves a total basic cost of £51,500 for the first child and £21,600 for each subsequent one. On top of this there can be the extras of independent school for, say, seven years costing some £32,000 for each child, and being a student for three years at some £2,600.

Of course, you may feel that your children will not cost as much as these figures suggest because you spend rather less in some areas, or because your circumstances are rather different. But there are other indirect costs not counted above. For example, the fact that you have children may mean that you decide on a larger home; you will be restricted to taking your holidays in the high season; the parent who stays away from work may well lose career progression, earning power and pension rights . . . and so it goes on.

The inescapable fact that children will cost you a lot is the reason for this book. Its aim is to bring together in one place all the information you are likely to need with regard to your children and money. It is arranged in roughly chronological order – roughly, because while the information and advice in a chapter may be most appropriate to one particular situation, it may also be helpful in others; and because the patterns of different people's lives are not the same. So while the book starts by looking at the kind of financial planning you can usefully do before you even start a family, you might find that much the same considerations – saving, buying a home, budgeting and borrowing – apply to you at other times after your children are born.

Chapter 2 looks more specifically at the financial side of having a baby – the benefits you can get from the State and the help you get from your firm if you have a job. Then comes a guide to all the kinds of assistance which the state provides to families – tax allowances, social security benefits, pension protection for people who stay at home to look after children, and so on. Lots of people who qualify for state benefits do not claim them, so if you find it hard to make ends meet it is worth checking whether there are any benefits you could claim. To find out if you qualify, check chapter 3.

The next chapter looks at the financial considerations when a marriage ends. No one could pretend that the arrangements which have to be made at this time are straightforward, and the financial ones may be the most complicated of all. But it is very important that the long-term arrangements made are financially sound, as this can literally save you thousands over the years.

Chapter 5 deals with money matters that apply to lone parents – whether single, separated, divorced or widowed – and also to couples who are not married to each other. These groups are dealt with together because, financially, they have a certain amount in common. There are a number of ways in which the financial arrangements they need to make are different from those of other people. In the past, the tax system tended to treat unmarried couples very favourably, but most of the advantages they had have now been removed. Moreover, there are ways in which the social security system is reputedly mean on unmarried couples, as it penalizes single people for living together but does not give a common-law wife the same benefits as a married woman (no wife's State pension or widow's benefits, for example).

Chapter 6 applies mainly to families where both parents work or where there is only one parent and he or she works. It covers the various ways in which children can be looked after while you are at work, including nursery schools, creches, childminders, nannies and au pairs.

The remaining chapters apply to anyone with children, whatever their circumstances. Chapter 7 looks at your children's money, whether this be in the form of gifts from relatives, pocket money, earnings from a Saturday job or whatever. It considers where children should put their savings, and then gives more detailed advice on the best ways of investing money for children for the long term. Saving just a fairly small amount on a regular basis for the first fifteen or twenty years of your child's life can mean that a substantial nest-egg builds up. But it is important to choose the investment scheme carefully, and take the various factors into account.

Chapter 8 asks you to consider what would happen to your children if you or your partner were to die or were unable to work for a long time due to illness, accident or disablement. You may already have very good protection in either event, but you may have very little. This chapter describes the varieties of insurance which can cover these eventualities and recommends the most economical types.

Chapter 9 covers everything to do with the costs involved in your children's education and the help you can get towards them. So it looks at the cost of uniforms, books, fares, outings, and so on. It shows why planning from a very early age will be necessary for most people who want to send their children to an independent school, and explains ways of financing this. It considers the grants and concessions you can get from the state at different stages of your child's education and the help you may get from your employer. It also looks at the financial position when children finish their education and venture into the world of work, training or, for some, unemployment.

Last, but certainly not least, chapter 10 covers the important business of passing on to your children the assets that you have built up during your lifetime. It explains inheritance tax and its consequences, looks at the implications of giving things away in your lifetime, explains why it is very important for anyone with a child to make a will and review it from time to time, and gives guidance on what your will should say.

It is hoped that, armed with the information in this book, you will be able to make sure that your financial arrangements are suited to your circumstances, that there are no aspects you have overlooked, that you are getting all the benefits you are entitled to, that you are getting good value for money from the financial services you pay for, and that you are making sound arrangements for your children's future.

The text of this book is based on the Government's proposals for taxation and social security for 1988–89, but at the time of going to press they had not become law and it is possible that there are minor variations.

1 Before the first baby

Many couples will find that their cash situation changes quite substantially once they start a family. Instead of two people living on two incomes there may well be three people living on one income – and the new arrival will require a fair amount of new equipment in the shape of prams, nappies, toys, bedding and clothing. The £750 total start-up costs suggested on page 7 derives from the following:

Maternity clothes	£120
Layette	£60
Baby's outer clothes	£50
Shoes	£20
Nappies and bucket	£25
Bottles, etc	£15
Bouncing cradle	£15
Cot and mattress	£80
Bedding	£40
Carrycot on wheels	£120
Pram linen	£20
Buggy-type pushchair	£50
Playpen	£45

High chair	£40
Bath	£10
Baby's car seat	£40
Total	£750

Of course, you may be able to acquire some of these from friends or buy them second-hand, but it is still likely that you will be laying out a fair bit of cash around the time of the baby's birth.

If you haven't yet started a family but are planning to do so, you may find yourselves in a financial dilemma. On the one hand, you may be reluctant to give up enjoying the spending power of two incomes – leading an active social life, having two holidays a year, running two cars, or whatever. Starting a family may mean that you will not have the same proportion of disposable income for maybe twenty years – so you may feel like making the most of it. On the other hand, you can undoubtedly ease the financial burden of the first few years of parenthood by foregoing some of the luxuries of your current responsibility-free life and looking ahead. There are, in fact, various useful preparations that you can make, and steps you can take to make the money go further.

Saving up

Before you start a family, it is well worth setting aside any spare cash you have to help out after the baby is born. If there are two of you on good salaries, you might be able to save £100 a month for two years in a building society, which at 6% interest will mount up to £2,555. Saving £50 a month for five years would give £3,500. This is quite a tidy sum, which you could draw on as and when needed. What you did not draw out would remain invested and continue to have interest added. Any money that you did not subsequently need to spend yourselves could form a useful start to your child's lifetime savings.

A building society is likely to be the best place for this kind of saving before your child is born. Interest rates are generally higher than those of banks, and with most types of account you can withdraw without giving any notice. It is probably worth going for an account with a high interest rate and no frills (like chequebooks or cashcards). The names of these accounts vary from one society to another but are often something like Gold Account or Premium Shares. If you want to save a fixed amount each month, or if it will not inconvenience you to give a month's or three months' notice of withdrawal, a special account based on one of these conditions is likely to pay you slightly more interest. Most building societies add the interest they pay to the money in your account – where it can itself earn interest – unless you specifically choose an account where the interest is paid out.

In some cases, you may get a higher return from a National Savings investment, available from post offices. If the person investing is single and doesn't pay tax, or if you are married and neither of you pays any tax, or if only the wife works and she earns less than £6,700, it is worth checking out the interest rates paid on the National Savings Investment Account and National Savings Deposit Bonds. Interest on these accounts is paid without any tax being deducted first, and if the account holder's income (including the interest from this account) isn't large enough for him to be liable to tax he won't have to pay any on the interest he gets. (Remember that at the moment a married woman counts as a taxpayer if her husband pays tax, though this is planned to change in April 1990.) With the Investment Account, you can pay money in at any time but must give a month's notice to withdraw. Deposit Bonds pay slightly more interest but are more restrictive in that deposits must be at least £100, withdrawals at least £50, and you have to give three months' notice to withdraw; any money withdrawn within a year only gets half the interest rate.

If you want to save regularly for five years or more, there are two specific schemes worth considering. You can save between

£1 and £20 a month in a Save-As-You-Earn (SAYE) scheme which many building societies run. This pays you a return of 8.3% a year tax-free if you save for 5 years. You can withdraw your money before that, but only get 6% interest. If, after the five years, you leave your money invested for a further two years, the return becomes 8.6% a year free of tax.

If you want to save between £20 and £200 a month, National Savings has a scheme called Yearly Plan which is available at post offices. For each Plan you make just 12 monthly payments which go to buy you a Certificate; if you keep the Certificate for four more years, it is repaid with interest which is currently equivalent to 7% a year tax-free over the five years. If you cash in the Certificate earlier you get less interest. You can of course continue saving for more than 12 months, in which case a new plan will be started and another Certificate bought at the end of the second year. Being tax-free, this investment provides a good return for higher-rate taxpayers.

You could consider going for a more glamorous investment than the simple building society or the schemes above. You might, for example, consider investing in 'gilts' (British Government stock). There are two ways to invest: through the National Savings Bonds & Stock Office (if you have £250 or more to invest) or through a bank or stockbroker (only worthwhile if you have £5,000 or more to invest). There is a large number of different stocks, most of which have a fixed redemption date – i.e. the day on which the government will repay the face value of the stock to the holder. Until then the government pays the holder interest at a fixed rate (the coupon) every six months. You can buy and sell stock at any time, but the price varies from day to day. Generally the price rises when bank interest rates fall and *vice versa*. So it is best to buy stock when interest rates are high and sell either when they have fallen (to make a short-term profit) or when the stock is redeemed (to get a guaranteed return). A few stocks are index-linked – i.e. both the interest payments and the redemption value are increased in line with the Retail Price Index (RPI).

Gilts are a reasonably safe investment, in that if you hold them until redemption you know exactly how much you are going to get back, and you may be able to get a higher return than this by selling beforehand. The main risk is that you will need to get your money back at a time when the price is low – in which case you could do rather badly. You can get a leaflet about the stocks which you can buy through the Bonds and Stock office from any post office, along with a form and envelope. If you want to buy a large amount of stock it would be worth asking your bank to recommend a stockbroker.

Alternatively, you might consider putting your money in a unit trust (many unit trusts have monthly savings schemes). Some have done extremely well in the past, producing a return two or three times higher than a building society, but you would be extremely lucky if you happened to choose one of the top-performing trusts out of the 300-odd around, though there is a reasonable chance of picking one which will beat a building society. However, unit trusts are not suitable for people wanting a guaranteed return for a specific purpose such as starting a new family. They often advertise their success in achieving a high rate of growth in a short period of time, but they are really long-term investments. In particular, you should remember that the value of units depends entirely on the value of the investments in the trust. These can fall as well as rise, so there is always the possibility of losing money. You can, of course, decrease the risk of doing badly by 'spreading' the money you invest between several unit trusts – although this also decreases your chance of doing particularly well overall.

You should not consider investing these sorts of savings in company shares unless you already have a substantial amount of money in safe investments like building societies and National Savings. The reason is that the costs of buying and selling small numbers of shares is comparatively high, so you need to have a large number of shares in a company to make it worthwhile. But it would be far too risky to put all your money into one company's shares, so you need to have shares in a number of companies – probably a dozen or more. This means that, apart from a small dabble in the privatization issues and a few small shareholdings you may have inherited, you should not consider a substantial investment in shares unless you have, say, £20,000 or more to invest. And at least a quarter of this should be invested where its capital value is safe.

As well as saving up to have some money to spend on your baby, you may also be wanting to start saving for the longer term – for example, to start building up savings for your child to have when he or she comes of age, or to pay for school fees or higher education. The most suitable forms of investment for these circumstances are described in chapters 7 and 9.

Your home and mortgage

If you aren't yet buying your own home but you intend to do so before long, it is worth trying to complete the house purchase well before the baby arrives. Apart from the practical reasons of not having to move home with a new baby, there are several financial reasons for this. First, house prices in most areas have risen almost continuously for a good many years, and there is no sign of this trend stopping. The earlier you can jump on to this particular bandwagon the better, as you will then be sharing in the profits.

Secondly, the amount of money you can borrow on a mortgage is generally a multiple of how much you and your partner earn. The maximum that most building societies and banks will lend is generally worked out as two and a half or three times the higher of your incomes, plus the other income. For example, if one of you earns £10,000 and the other £8,000, you may be able to borrow up to 2½ times £10,000 (which is £25,000) plus £8,000, which comes to £33,000. If only one of you is working after the baby is expected or born and you apply for a mortgage then, you won't be able to borrow as much. However, it would be sensible to exercise some caution:

if you borrow the maximum on two incomes, you may find it hard to manage when one of you stops earning.

Finally, the fact that you are likely to borrow a large part of the cost of your home multiplies the return you get on your investment. For example, suppose you buy a £30,000 home with savings of £5,000 and a mortgage of £25,000, and sell it six years later for £40,000, when you still owe £22,000. You have turned your £5,000 investment into £18,000 – a very handsome return. Of course it's often only a notional gain, because you are likely to want to use most of the money you get to buy your next home – but this money will allow you to trade up to a bigger and better home than you could otherwise have afforded.

However, to be able to afford a home at all there are two essentials. You must be able to afford the mortgage repayments fairly comfortably, and you must have saved up enough for a deposit. Even if you are lucky enough to get a 100% mortgage (i.e. borrow the whole of the purchase price) there are still costs associated with buying a home (like surveyor's and solicitor's fees) which will run into several hundred pounds, and you are likely to need some money for decorating and furnishing. If you are not in this position yet, you may have no alternative but to wait.

Your mortgage

If you have bought your home with a repayment mortgage (not an endowment loan), an effective way of saving is simply to repay more of your loan than you have to. Anything extra you pay goes to reduce the amount you owe the lender, so that the monthly repayments you have to make in the future will be lower.

For example, suppose you and your partner have bought a home with a £30,000 mortgage over 25 years. You are both working, and you hope to start a family in a few years time. If the mortgage interest rate is 10%, your monthly repayments will be about £225. You reckon you can afford to pay rather more than this, and decide to pay the lender £350 a month. After five years you decide to start your family, and there will only be one full-time income. The amount you now owe on the mortgage is only about £18,700 instead of £27,400. This means that your monthly repayments for the remaining 20 years of the mortgage would be only £153 a month instead of £225 – a saving of over £70 a month (this assumes the same interest rate right through).

Some lenders have set schemes for paying more in the early years of a mortgage and less in later ones – called 'high-start' mortgages. But almost any lender will be happy to accept extra payments at any time.

If your mortgage is from a building society, you would do best to make a slightly different arrangement, because of the way that building societies work out the interest due on a mortgage. First, find out when the end of the building society's accounting year is (if you have already had an annual mortgage statement, it will be the end of the last month shown on that). Now instead of making higher monthly payments to your mortgage account, open a savings account and make your monthly payments into that. Then each year, a couple of weeks before the end of the mortgage accounting year, withdraw your savings and pay the money into your mortgage account.

The reason for this is that building societies charge interest each year on the amount that you owe at the beginning of that year. If you pay off extra during the course of the year, you get no benefit until the start of the next year. But if you pay extra money into your mortgage account just before the end of the accounting year, you get the benefit for the whole of the following year, and that money will in the meantime have been accumulating interest in the savings account.

Other loans and credit cards

If you have any other loans (apart from your mortgage) or you owe money from previous months on a credit card, it will be worth using any spare cash you have to pay off these loans. The reason is that the interest rate on most loans is pretty high – often 20% to 40% a year. This is much higher than the interest rate you can get by investing money, so it is nearly always worth withdrawing savings to pay off such loans. The only exceptions are interest-free loans or if the interest rate is very low (under 8%, say) as may be the case with certain special car loans and certain insurance policy loans. In these cases only pay the loan off early if you want to be shot of the monthly repayments.

Budgeting for when your income will be lower

If you are used to having enough ready cash for most things you want to buy or do, you could well find the situation is rather different after the baby arrives. And if you have not found it easy to make ends meet while you have been childless, it will be even more important to keep a watchful eye on your finances. Most of us will not have felt the need to keep too close a check on our income and outgoings, but with the financial changes about to happen this can be a vital thing to do. There are several things you can do to help you keep in control of your money, and it is worth trying these out and developing new habits before the baby arrives.

As a first step, it is worth being clear about what you are trying to do. For example, your main objectives may be to have enough ready money for the bills you are expecting and the things you need to buy; to have some extra money you can get at quickly for unexpected bills (like garage bills, maintenance or repair bills, extra heating in a bad winter); and to have any other spare money saved where it will earn a good rate of interest.

First the bills. Most of us have to contend with something like this lot:

yearly
insurance premiums
car tax, MOT and
  AA/RAC membership
television licence
service agreements
season ticket
Christmas spending
birthday presents
holiday

half-yearly
water rates
car service
dentist

other periodical payments
coal, oil, bottled gas for heating
clothes
hairdresser
help in the home
fares to work

quarterly
electricity
gas
telephone
bank charges

monthly
mortgage or rent
rates instalments (or Poll Tax)
credit card payments
loan repayments
HP or rental payments
shop accounts
insurance instalments
newspapers

You can spread some of these bills more evenly over the year by paying in monthly instalments. You should always pay the rates on your home in monthly instalments because there is no extra charge at all for doing so. Don't ever borrow money or use a credit card to pay your rates. In Scotland your rates instalments will cover the water rates as well, but in England and Wales there is likely to be an extra charge for paying your water rates by instalments. Most insurance companies allow you to pay insurance premiums in instalments for a small extra charge. And you can arrange to pay your estimated bills for the next year for the phone or the electricity by twelve equal monthly instalments from your bank current account. If you overpay or underpay, you settle up at the end of the year.

A salutary exercise is to work out how much general spending money you have once all the regular bills and unavoidable payments have been settled. It is worth doing these sums for your present situation, and then seeing how much difference there will be once the baby arrives. First, calculate how much money you get in a year, by multiplying your monthly pay cheque by 12 or weekly one by 52 (use the amount of money you actually get, after tax and everything else has been deducted). Add on the total amount of Child Benefit or any other Social Security benefit or other income you get over the year. Then work out how much all the bills come to over a year (add up the monthly ones and multiply by 12, etc). Subtract this figure from your total income figure and divide by 52. The answer you get is the cash you have left to spend on other things each week.

Example

INCOME
Pay (12 × £750)   £9,000
Child Benefit (52 × £7.25)   £377

TOTAL INCOME OVER YEAR
                                                                   £9,377

PAYMENTS
yearly
   holiday   £600
   Christmas spending £200
   birthday presents   £100
   season ticket   £450
   car tax and MOT   £125
   television licence   £65
                                  =   £1,540

half-yearly
   water rates   £65
   car service   £60
   dentist   £25
                      £150 × 2 =   £300

quarterly

electricity	£70			
gas	£40			
telephone	£65			
	£175	× 4	=	£700

monthly

mortgage	£180			
rates	£45			
loan repayments	£30			
insurance instalments	£25			
newspapers	£12			
	£292	× 12	=	£3,504

other periodical payments

coal	£50	a year		
clothes	£350	a year		
hairdresser	£70	a year		
			=	£470

TOTAL PAYMENTS: **£6,514**
WHICH LEAVES: **£2,863**
CASH TO SPEND EACH WEEK: =   **£55**
(£2,863 divided by 52)

If you find budgeting difficult, one way to limit your spending is simply to withdraw this amount from your bank or building society account each week and pay for everything in cash (except the bills you have already allowed for). If you have to write a cheque, you must deduct the amount from next week's cash withdrawal. This system can also be a useful one to operate for a short time to get out of a tight period – after a holiday for example.

Keeping track of your money

Here is a useful way of keeping track of how much money you have. It is very useful to get into the habit of using a simple system like this before the baby arrives, particularly if you do not find it easy to balance the books at present. It will make sure you don't forget about regular bills and, if you use a bank current account or deposit account or a building society account, will make sure you don't forget about standing orders and direct debits. And you will know at any moment how much you can safely spend without overdrawing the account and incurring charges – without having to ask for the balance or wait for your monthly or quarterly statement.

All you need is a spare pocket diary, the cheapest you can find (they are often reduced in price after mid-January). A diary with a page or double-page to each week is ideal. Starting from the current week, draw two vertical lines down each page and head the three columns *In*, *Out* and *Balance*. You then go through the diary writing (in the *In* column) the amounts of all regular payments you expect to receive (salary, child benefit, freelance earnings, etc) on the dates you expect them. Then in the *Out* column put in all the standing orders and direct debits that will be made out of your account during the rest of the year. Then check when any other regular bills need paying – the gas, electricity, phone, rates instalments, water rates, credit card statements – and write in the expected amounts and what they are for. Write in family birthdays, Christmas spending, when you will have to pay for your holiday and when you will need to draw your holiday spending money. In each case make a realistic guess as to what the outlay will be.

Now you will need to know how much you have in your account at the moment. Either ask for a statement (or wait for your next one) and check it to see which of the payments you have made and money you have received have cleared through the account. Add to this any amounts paid into your account since, and subtract any payments which you know are on their way out (e.g. cheques you have written). Enter the figure that is left in the *Balance* column of your diary for today. From now on, whenever you pay money into your account or write a cheque, write the amount in the *In* or *Out* column for that day. And whenever there is a figure in the *In* or *Out* column, work out how much money is now in your account and write the figure in the *Balance* column. You can now see at a glance how much you have in your account. And you have an instant reminder of all the other payments which will go in and out of your account automatically, so it is easy to see how much money you can safely withdraw without the risk of overdrawing or becoming liable for bank charges.

A more thorough way to budget and plan your spending is to draw up a yearly budget plan. You will need a large sheet of paper with one wide column and 12 narrower ones, headed with the names of the months. In the wide column you list your sources of income and the things you spend it on. The very top line of each monthly column shows the balance brought forward from the previous month. In each monthly column, this balance is added to the total income for the month, and the total expenses are deducted, leaving the balance to be carried forward in the bottom line. This figure is copied to the top line of the next column, as the starting balance for the next month, and so on. If you have a home computer, you may be able to get a program called a 'spreadsheet' with a table like this already set up. The advantage of this is that you can make guesses at future amounts to get an estimate of how much spare cash you will have in the future. Then when you know the exact amounts, you can change any of the figures and the program will automatically recalculate any other figures which depend on it (such as the monthly totals and balances). This saves you a lot of time with a pencil and rubber.

2 Baby benefits

You are not entirely on your own in having to meet the costs of the addition to your family. A working mother may be able to get financial help from her employer as well as having rights concerning maternity leave and returning to her job. Mothers who are unemployed or do not qualify for help from their employers can get some help from the State.

Statutory Maternity Pay

This is money which your employer has to pay you for 18 weeks of your maternity leave, providing certain conditions are met. If you don't qualify, you may be able to get a State benefit called maternity allowance instead – see below.

You should get statutory maternity pay (SMP) from your employer if you have been in your job for at least six months up to the 26th week of your pregnancy (15 weeks before the baby is due), and if on average you earn at least £41 a week.

SMP will be paid for 18 weeks (even if your baby is premature) if you claim between 11 and six weeks before the baby is due. If you work after the start of the sixth week you'll lose SMP for those weeks. If your baby is born more than 11 weeks before the expected date, SMP will be paid from the following week. You are still entitled to SMP even if your baby is stillborn (as long as your pregnancy lasted 28 weeks or more) or dies before the end of the 18 weeks.

For the first six weeks SMP will be paid at a rate of nine tenths of your normal weekly pay if you've worked for your employer for two years or more (five years or more if you normally work for eight to 16 hours a week). For the remaining weeks it will be paid at a lower rate of £34.25. If you've worked for less than two (or five) years, you'll get the lower rate throughout. Any tax and National Insurance contributions payable will be deducted from what you get. This is the minimum amount required by law – your employer's policy may be to pay more (though the extra may be dependent on your returning to work after your baby's birth).

You have to tell your employer that you intend to stop work to have a baby at least 21 days before you leave (or as soon as reasonably practical). Your employer can ask for this in writing and can ask for medical evidence of your expected date of birth, such as your maternity certificate.

If your employer decides that you do not qualify for SMP, he or she should give you a form SMP.1 saying why. You will need this in order to claim any state help. If you think the decision is wrong, you can ask your local social security office to decide.

For full details of SMP, see leaflet NI.17A available from your local social security office or clinic. Your post office or library may also have copies.

State benefits

Maternity allowance

If you can't get SMP, you may be able to get maternity allowance. This is a tax-free social security benefit, currently paid at a rate of £31.30 per week. You can also claim extra benefit of £19.40 for your husband or anyone else looking after your other children if they earn less than £19.40 per week.

To get maternity allowance you must have been working and paid full National Insurance contributions for at least six months out of the 12 months up to the 26th week of your pregnancy. If you don't qualify, you may be able to get sickness benefit for part of the time you are pregnant. You should claim maternity allowance in any case – if you don't qualify your claim will automatically be considered for sickness benefit and you won't have to make a separate claim.

You can get the allowance for up to 18 weeks starting from the 11th week before the baby is due (or the week after the birth if the baby is very premature and born earlier than this). If you work longer than the end of the seventh week before it is due, your allowance will be reduced by one week for each week or part week you work. You should claim it as soon as possible after the 14th week before the baby is due, even if you are working. If you claim late, you may not get any allowance for some or all of the weeks gone by. You are still entitled to the allowance even if your baby is stillborn (as long as your pregnancy lasted 28 weeks or more) or dies.

Send a copy of your maternity certificate (from your doctor or midwife) with your claim form. If you are working but not entitled to statutory maternity pay, your employer must give you form SMP.1 – send this too.

Sickness and invalidity benefits

If you are still employed by your employer when your SMP ends, and you are incapable of work, you may be entitled to statutory sick pay (SSP) from him or her (see p.113). If you are not entitled to SSP you can claim sickness benefit. You will need form SSP.1E from your employer to do this.

If you are unemployed when your SSP or maternity allowance runs out, and incapable of work, you can claim sickness benefit using form SC.1 (see p.115). When this runs out, you can claim invalidity benefit if you are still unable to work.

Lump sum maternity payment from the Social Fund
If you are receiving income support (see p.44) or family credit (see p.43) when your baby is due, you can claim a lump sum payment of £85 from the Social Fund (see p.51). But it will be reduced by £1 for every £1 that your savings are over £500. You must claim between 11 weeks before the baby is born and three months after, using form SF.100.

Other benefits
During your pregnancy and for a year after your child's birth, you are entitled to free medicines on NHS prescriptions and free NHS dental treatment.

For free prescriptions, ask your doctor, midwife or health visitor for a form FW.8. But if you have already had your baby, get DHSS leaflet P.11 from your local social security office or post office and use form A attached. You can get free medicines for your child from birth to 16 simply by filling in the back of the prescription form before handing it to the chemist.

For free dental treatment, simply tell the dentist you are pregnant or have had a baby in the last 12 months. You will be asked to sign a form confirming this.

If your income is low, there may be further benefits you can claim. Details are in the next chapter, which also gives more information on child benefit, one-parent benefit and other benefits for children.

A useful guide to all the benefits available is the DHSS free leaflet FB.8 *Babies and Benefits* which contains a helpful checklist on what you should do at various stages of your pregnancy and after your baby is born.

Benefits for working women

In addition to 18 weeks' Statutory Maternity Pay (see p.25), many working women expecting a baby have a right to take time off work for ante-natal care, to take 39 weeks off work for the birth and to return to their job at the end of that period.

The benefits described here are the minimum laid down by law. Many trade unions have negotiated better maternity benefits than this, so check what benefits your firm offers. For example, some employers have agreed on shorter qualifying periods, maternity leave up to a year, and maternity pay for up to 40 weeks. Some firms offer paternity leave as well, and a few will allow you to return to work up to five years later.

Time off work for ante-natal care

You have a right to attend ante-natal check-ups, whether at hospital, health centre or GP's surgery during working hours without losing any pay, provided that you have an appointment. For the first appointment you should tell your employer why you are taking the time off and how long you expect to be away from work. For subsequent appointments your employer can ask to see your appointment card and pregnancy certificate. Your firm is entitled to ask you to arrange appointments as far as possible at times which are convenient for your work, but if it refuses to let you attend the sessions or refuses to pay you at your normal rate for the time you take off, you have grounds for a complaint to an industrial tribunal – this is an informal court for hearing disputes between employers and employees.

Can you lose your job?

When you have worked for your firm for a certain time, your employers cannot sack you because of your pregnancy or anything which results from it. If they did, you could in most cases claim unfair dismissal and have your case heard by an industrial tribunal.

You have this right if you have worked for the firm for one year or more. But if the firm has not employed more than 20 people during the whole time you have worked for it, you only get this right after working for the firm for two years. If you normally work less than 16 hours a week you have to wait five years (but if you normally work less than 8 hours a week, you don't ever acquire this right). In each case 'working for the firm' means continuous employment with the same company or a connected company (such as one that is a subsidiary of the other, or that takes it over). A previous maternity leave, after which you returned to work with the same employer, counts towards your period of continuous employment. If you are a teacher, working in different schools for the same local authority counts as continuous employment. If you have spent some of the time on a Government training scheme, check whether the time counts towards your period of continuous employment – some schemes do not (for example, time spent on a Youth Training Scheme counts if you were an employee but not if you were a trainee).

Even if you pass the tests above, there are still two circumstances where you could lose your job. If your pregnancy means you cannot do your job adequately (perhaps because it involves lifting heavy boxes), or if it is illegal for a pregnant woman to do your job (because you are a radiologist, for example), your employer must offer you any other suitable job he has available which you could do, on rates of pay and conditions which are generally as good as those in your normal job. If you turn down his offer, or if there is no suitable alternative job to offer you, you cannot claim unfair dismissal if your employer dismisses you.

However, you do not lose your rights to maternity pay and to return to work at the end of your maternity leave provided that, if you had not lost your job, you would have satisfied all the normal conditions (see below). But to preserve the right to return to work, you must also tell your employer when you leave the job that you do intend to return.

Maternity leave

You can take maternity leave from the beginning of the 11th week before the week in which your baby is due. If you leave any earlier than this, unless it's due to a premature birth, you forfeit both your right to any maternity pay at all and your right to get your job back again. So if you are not well enough to work, take sick leave but do not leave the job. You can, however, stay on at your job after the 11th week before the expected birth if you want to – but if you work beyond the sixth week, you lose statutory maternity pay for those weeks.

You may find when you take your maternity leave that the firm treats you as though you had left permanently. Even if it still regards you as an employee, you don't have any legal right to any employee benefits, though some employers extend certain benefits to women on maternity leave. Also it is not illegal for your firm to advertise your job as though it was a permanent vacancy. None of these factors need concern you too much, as they do not affect your rights to maternity pay or to return to work.

Returning to work

Provided you meet certain conditions, you have a right to return to your job at any time within 29 weeks of the beginning of the week in which the baby is born. The pay and conditions you get must be as good as they would have been if you had been at work the whole time (so you must be given any pay rises the rest of the work force have had). However, you can't necessarily return if there are five or fewer employees in all, or if it's not reasonably practical to offer you your former job or a suitable alternative.

The conditions for qualifying are that you must have worked for the firm for two years or more (five years or more if you normally work for 8 to 16 hours per week). You must also tell your employer *in writing* that you intend to stop work to have a baby, and your letter must also give the expected date of birth and say that you intend to return to work after your maternity leave.

Your employer may write to you after your baby is born to ask if you still want to go back to work. If you do, you must write and say so within 14 days (or as soon as is reasonably practicable). If you have not yet decided, say that you intend to return – otherwise you will lose your right to do so.

You must write again to your employer giving at least 21 days' notice of your intention to return to work. So your last chance to make up your mind is 26 weeks after the beginning of the week in which your baby was born (write this down in a diary or calendar that you use regularly, so you don't forget, or get your partner to do it and remind you). At this point you must write saying whether you intend to return at the beginning of the 29th week. Your employer can postpone your starting date for up to four weeks, but must tell you why. If you are ill at the time you are due to go back to work, your return can be put off for up to four weeks as long as you have a medical certificate.

If you decide that you do not want to return to your job you are free to do so; contrary to what some people think, you do not have to repay any of the maternity pay or benefit you have received.

Problems with maternity benefits

If you need further information about any of the above rights, ask for the free leaflet *Employment Rights for the Expectant Mother* at your local Jobcentre or unemployment office. If you disagree about the amount of any payment or the length of time you have worked for the firm, ask for the leaflet *Rules Governing Continuous Employment and a Week's Pay*. If you think you are being denied any of your rights and perhaps have a case for an Industrial Tribunal, you should first get in touch with your regional office of the Advisory, Conciliation and Arbitration Service (ACAS). The addresses and phone numbers of these are listed in the back of the booklets mentioned above. You can simply phone to make an appointment for a 45-minute discussion of your case with an experienced counsellor who will advise you on the steps to take in your circumstances (you should take any relevant papers with you). Do not delay, as complaints have to be made within three months. All ACAS services are completely free and impartial. Your local Jobcentre, library or Citizens Advice Bureau may have copies of the leaflets *Conciliation between Individuals and Employers* and *Industrial Tribunals Procedure* which explain the steps involved.

3 State help for families

There are a number of ways in which the state helps parents with the cost of providing for children. The state also provides extra income and help with housing costs for families on lower incomes. It seems that many families do not realise they qualify for these benefits as large numbers do not claim – so it is well worth checking whether you qualify.

This chapter concentrates on arrangements for married couples and their children; special considerations for one-parent families and for unmarried couples with children are given in chapter 5.

Help for married couples

Your tax allowances
At the present time, a married man can have a higher amount of income than a single man before he starts paying tax. In the 1988–89 tax year, a married man gets a tax allowance of £4,095, whereas a single man pays tax on earnings above £2,605. Although called the married man's tax allowance, either husband or wife can benefit from it as it can be set against any of their income – so if the husband earns less than

£4,095 the remainder of the allowance can be set against his wife's earnings or any of the couple's income from investments. At first sight, it seems that married men are getting a helping hand towards the cost of maintaining a family. But this is not necessarily the case, because of the allowance given to his wife.

A wife's tax allowance is the same amount as the single person's allowance, but it can only be set against her earnings, not against any income from her investments. Nor can it be transferred to her husband. This means that if you are both working, you can have up to £6,700 free of tax between you (in the 1988-89 tax year). But if the wife stops work, you not only lose one income but you lose the wife's allowance too — so only £4,095 of the husband's earnings are free of tax.

A side effect of this system is that (assuming husband and wife earned the same) you would actually pay less tax if it were the wife who went out to work and the husband who stayed at home to look after the children. This is because the husband's allowance can be transferred to the wife — so she can earn up to £6,700 before she pays any tax. (Any husband who does this should arrange with the DHSS to protect his right to a state pension; a wife gets this protection automatically — see p.108).

Until 1989, it is still the case that an unmarried couple with children may pay less tax than a married couple with children. However, the difference is less than it was, and it is planned to change the way that married couples are taxed from 6 April 1990. After that date it is planned that husband and wife will each be taxed independently. Each will have a personal allowance (identical to a single person's allowance) which can be set against any of his or her income, whether it comes from earnings or investments. If one partner doesn't work or earns less than the amount of their allowance, the rest of his or her allowance will be lost — it cannot be given to the spouse. However, a married couple will also get a married couple's allowance, which will be equal to the difference between the current married man's allowance and single person's allowance. This allowance will normally be set against the husband's income, but if his income is too low to use it all the unused part will be transferred to his wife to set against her income.

Most married couples will pay the same amount of tax under this system as they would under the current system. There are three main differences. First, a wife's income will no longer be counted as her husband's. She will be responsible for filling in her own Tax Return and paying her own tax, and there will be no need for her husband to have any knowledge of her income. Second, married women who earn less than the amount of the single person's allowance but who have some investment income which is currently taxed as their husband's income will find that less tax is payable on this investment income. Last, there will be no advantage in the wife going out to work and the husband staying at home to look after the children.

Being taxed separately
Couples with high earnings may be able to save substantial amounts of tax by asking to have the wife's earnings taxed separately, but the combined income has to be large – in 1988–89 at least £28,484. You will need to work out at the end of the tax year how much tax would be payable with this option and how much without it – and plump for whichever means less to pay. Details are in Inland Revenue leaflet IR.13 *Wife's Earnings Election*, which is available free from tax offices. You can do this up to two years after the end of the relevant tax year.

This option will end when the planned changes are introduced in April 1990, but higher earning couples will in any case pay less tax than they would under the current system.

Pension situation of the parent at home

One way that a parent who stays at home to look after children has lost out against a working parent is that he or she has not been building up a pension entitlement. But in 1987 this

STATE HELP FOR FAMILIES

position was improved, and you may not now lose any entitlement to a state basic pension.

Generally, you need to pay National Insurance contributions for around nine tenths of your working life – generally this means paying contributions for 44 years for a man, 39 for a woman – to get the full amount of basic pension. Class 1 contributions (which are deducted from your pay from a job), Class 2 (paid by the self-employed) and Class 3 (voluntary contributions) all count equally, and you can combine the three types over your working life.

There are also circumstances in which you can be credited with National Insurance contributions instead of having to pay them – for example if you're claiming unemployment benefit or receiving maternity allowance.

If you stay at home to look after children, you don't get NI credits but you'll probably qualify for Home Responsibilities Protection (HRP) which means your state basic pension doesn't suffer through not paying NI contributions. Each year for which you get HRP reduces the number of qualifying years you need for a basic pension – though to get the full amount of pension you must have paid (or been credited with) NI contributions totalling at least 20 qualifying years, and the rest of your working life must be covered by HRP. If your total is less than this, your basic pension will be reduced.

You automatically get HRP for a year if you receive child benefit for a child under 16 for the whole of that tax year (from 6 April one year to 5 April the next). Child benefit is normally paid to the mother, but if the mother works and the father stays at home to look after the children, it is better if the benefit is paid to him so that his pension is protected. There are two other (unusual) circumstances in which you can claim HRP – see DHSS leaflet NP.27.

There is one exception to all this. If you are a married woman who has kept the right to pay National Insurance contributions at the reduced rate (often called the *lower stamp*) you do not get HRP and you do not have any entitlement to a state basic pension on your own contributions.

All married women are also entitled to a wife's state pension based on their husband's National Insurance contributions. If when you reach retirement age you qualify for both a wife's state pension and a pension on your own contributions, you normally get whichever is higher.

For each child

Child benefit
For each child under the age of 16 (or 19 if the child is still in full-time education other than higher education) the mother receives a regular payment known as child benefit. In 1988–89 the amount is £7.25 a week. Every mother is entitled to this, irrespective of income and situation, provided only that the child is living with her (or that she contributes towards the child's maintenance) and that at the time of claiming she has lived in Britain for half the previous year. To claim child benefit, get forms CH.2 and CH.3 from a social security office.

It is possible for child benefit to be paid to the father instead of the mother – if she doesn't want to claim it for herself or, if it is the father who stays home to look after the children, to protect his state pension.

Child benefit is now normally paid every four weeks in arrears, either by orders you cash at a post office or by being paid direct into a bank or building society account. But if you qualify for one-parent benefit or if you or your partner get family credit or income support, you can ask to have your child benefit paid weekly. You can also apply if you are finding it very hard to manage with the benefit paid four-weekly.

Further details of child benefit are in DHSS leaflets CH.1, CH.4, CH.5, CH.6 and CH.7.

If you look after other children
If you look after a child who is not your own and you get child benefit for him or her, you may be able to get guardian's

allowance as well. This is a tax-free weekly payment of £8.40 for each such child, and it is paid in addition to the child benefit for the child or children.

You must support the child financially, but you do not have to be the legal guardian. You cannot claim the allowance if you have adopted the child, unless you were receiving or were entitled to get the allowance for the child immediately before the adoption.

One of the child's parents must be dead and the other either dead, unknown, untraceable, in prison for a long period or under no obligation to maintain the child. One of the child's parents must also have been born in Great Britain or have lived here for a certain period.

Further details are in DHSS leaflet NI.14, and you claim the allowance on form BG.1.

Health and welfare benefits

Children under 16 do not have to pay for prescribed medicines, nor for dental treatment. To get these free you simply sign the declaration on the prescription or the dentist's form. The same applies to women who have had a baby in the last 12 months, except that to get free prescriptions they must apply on form P.11 for an exemption certificate.

Children under 16, and those under 19 who are in full-time education, are entitled to NHS vouchers for glasses or contact lenses. If you wish to buy glasses which are more expensive than the value of the voucher, you will have to pay the extra yourself. To claim, ask the optician for form F.1 and send it to the social security office. Details are in DHSS leaflet G.11, *NHS Vouchers for Glasses*.

Other members of families who get family credit or income support can also get these benefits free (see p.51). Families with incomes which are low but not quite low enough to qualify for family credit or income support may be entitled to free or reduced value dental treatment or vouchers for glasses. The mother in a family with a low income can also get free milk and vitamins for herself while she is pregnant and for her children under school age. Details and how to claim are in DHSS leaflet MV.11.

Housing benefit

The housing benefit scheme can provide help with your rates and rent. If you have children under 18 living at home you can qualify for benefit more easily and get a larger amount than most people without children.

The scheme is basically a standard one run by local councils in all areas. Large numbers of families who are entitled to housing benefit do not claim it, possibly because they think their income is too high, or perhaps because the scheme is very complicated or not sufficiently well publicized. How you claim housing benefit and what you get depends on whether or not you get income support (see p.44), but you don't have to be getting income support to claim housing benefit. However, you can't claim if you live with a close relative and you pay rent or rates to them, nor if you have £8,000 or more in savings.

If you're getting income support you'll automatically qualify for housing benefit to cover the full amount of your rent, and 80 per cent of your rates. Your income support is supposed to cover 20 per cent of your rates, and your water rates. If you're an owner-occupier, it should also cover your mortgage interest payments (but only half of them for the first 16 weeks), interest on existing home improvement loans and any ground rent or service charge you have to pay.

If you're not getting income support, you may still qualify for rent and rate rebates, but you will get nothing towards mortgage interest, water rates or the portion of your rates not covered by housing benefit, however low your income is. Whether you qualify, and how much housing benefit you get depends on your income (after tax and National Insurance contributions), the amount of your savings, the composition of

STATE HELP FOR FAMILIES

your family and your housing costs. The council will work out whether your net income after tax and National Insurance contributions (including child benefit, family credit and most other state benefits) is more than the amount you'd be entitled to under income support – known as the 'applicable amount'. Any savings you have between £3,000 and £8,000 are taken into account as well – for every £250 above £3,000 you'll be assumed to have an income of £1 per week. As a guide, in 1988–89, the applicable amount for a couple (one working) with two children aged between 11 and 15, and savings of less than £3,000, would be £89.90 per week. That's equivalent to take-home pay of £79.90 per week (the first £5 of each partner's earnings are ignored, but child benefit of £15 per week counts as income too) or to £346.23 per month. See p.46 for how income support rates are calculated.

If your income is less than or equal to the applicable amount, you'll get housing benefit to cover all your rent and 80 per cent of your rates. If your income is more than the applicable amount, then your rent rebate will be reduced by 65 per cent of the difference, and your rate rebate by 20 per cent of the difference. So, if your housing costs are high, you may qualify for something even if your income is not particularly low – for example, even if your income exceeded the applicable amount by £100 per week you could still get something if your rent was more than £65 per week.

Whether you are on income support or not, your housing benefit will be reduced if you have anyone living in your home who is not dependent on you (for example, a grown-up child or a lodger). It may also be reduced if the council considers your home unreasonably large or expensive (though this won't apply if there is a young child, a person with disabilities or someone over 60 living in the house), or if part of the house is used for business purposes, or if you pay service charges to your landlord which are optional (i.e. not part of your tenancy) or for personal services, such as meals or food, or personal cleaning and laundry.

Because the housing benefit scheme is a fairly complicated one, the golden rule is to apply if you think there is any possibility of being eligible. Ask at your council offices (or library or Citizens Advice Bureau) for leaflets RR.1 *Help with Rent and Rates* and RR.2 *A Guide to Housing Benefit*, and for an application form (one form usually covers both rent and rate rebates).

Apply direct to the council if you are not on income support – but if you think you might be entitled to income support (see p.44) claim this instead at your local social security office and you will automatically be considered for housing benefit at the same time. Don't be put off by a long application form for housing benefit – ask for help at your local Citizens Advice Bureau if you need help filling it in. The council will work out if you qualify, and, if so, how much you are entitled to. You should be told the result of your application within 14 days, but in some areas there is a backlog of applications which may mean it is some time before you hear anything.

If you get housing benefit and there is any change in your circumstances (including having another child, or a child leaving home or getting a job), you should let the council know and they will recalculate the amount of benefit you are entitled to. When the period of your rebate ends you will need to apply for a continuation – do so within a month if possible in order to receive the rebate without a break.

How housing benefit is paid depends on whether you rent or own your home. If you live in council accommodation, the rent and rates you pay will be reduced. If you live in privately rented accommodation, your rates will be reduced and the council will send you the money towards your rent, unless you normally pay both rent and rates to your landlord, in which case the council will send you both rebates.

If you own your own home, your monthly rates instalment will be reduced, or, if you have already paid your rates, you will get a refund. If you continue to qualify in future years, your rates bill or instalments will be reduced.

For working parents

Family credit

If you have a family and are on a low income you can have your income topped up by family credit. Married couples, unmarried couples and single parents can all claim, as long as at least one parent works for at least 24 hours per week, and you don't have savings of more than £6,000. You must have at least one dependent child under 16 (or under 19 if still at school). You do not have to have paid any N I contributions.

While you receive family credit, your family also get free prescriptions and dental treatment, and are entitled to NHS vouchers for glasses. You may also qualify for some payments from the Social Fund (see p.51). Large numbers of people do not realise that they are entitled to these benefits and do not claim them – so it is well worth checking that you aren't amongst them.

Family credit is paid at different rates according to your income. If your income is at or below a set amount you'll get the maximum for a family of your size. If your income is above the limit, your family credit is reduced by 70 per cent of the excess. For 1988–89, the limit is £51.45 (whatever the size of your family).

The maximum amount of family credit for 1988–89 is £32.10 for the parents (this amount is the same whether there are one or two parents), plus £6.05 for each child under 11, £11.40 for each child aged 11 to 15, £14.70 for each child aged 16–17, and £21.35 for each child aged 18.

Your income for family credit is your net earnings after paying tax and National Insurance contributions and half of any contributions to a pension scheme, averaged over the five weeks before you claim (your net profits averaged over 26 weeks if you're self-employed). Include any maintenance payments you get. The DHSS will also assume an income of £1 for every £250 of savings you have over £3,000. Child benefit, mobility or attendance allowance and housing benefit don't count as income for family credit – but any family credit you receive will count as income for housing benefit (see p.41). The first 13 weeks of statutory sick pay and statutory maternity pay won't be counted as income.

If you qualify for family credit, the same weekly amount is paid to you for 26 weeks, regardless of any changes in your income or circumstances, or in the set amounts. The money you get is tax-free. It can be paid to you in two ways: direct into a bank or building society account every four weeks or by an order book which can be cashed weekly at a post office. The order book will be made out to the woman in a two-parent family, with the man named as the alternative payee.

To claim family credit, pick up leaflet FC.1 at a post office or local social security office. Fill in and send off the form enclosed. All family credit claims are dealt with by post – you don't have to go to a social security office. When you claim family credit for the first time, the DHSS will write to your employer for details of your earnings – you should not send payslips with the form. However, when you renew your claim your payslips will be sufficient evidence of earnings. If you're self-employed you'll need to send evidence of your business profits for the last six months with your claim.

Family credit replaced family income supplement (FIS) from 11 April 1988. If you were already getting FIS you will now get family credit instead – but it will not be less than the amount of FIS you were receiving.

For people with not enough to live on

Income support

Income support is a topping-up benefit for people who are not in full-time work – such as the unemployed, pensioners, people with disabilities, single parents and other people who cannot work because of responsibilities at home. It replaced supplementary benefit as the 'safety net' for people on low incomes from 11 April 1988. While it is not especially for families, having children will mean you qualify more easily and get a higher amount of benefit.

You qualify if your weekly income is less than the Government thinks someone in your circumstances needs to live on. Income support makes up the difference between the two. Most of the money you have coming in each week counts as income, whether it's from part-time earnings, maintenance payments or social security benefits or pensions.

You don't have to have paid any National Insurance contributions to claim income support. But there are two cases in which you cannot claim. The first is if you or your partner work an average of 24 hours or more a week. Looking after children at home does not count as work, nor does being on an MSC, JTS or YTS training scheme for which you get a training allowance. If you are off work because of sickness or have been laid off temporarily this is not counted as full-time work either. You may be able to claim income support while working more than 24 hours per week if you are disabled and only earning three-quarters or less of what you'd get if you were fit, or if you work at home as a childminder.

The second is if you have a total of more than £6,000 in cash, bank or building society accounts, or other savings and investments. The value of your own home won't be counted towards this total, nor the value of personal possessions (unless the DHSS thinks they have been bought deliberately to bring your capital down). Money you get from selling your home which you intend to use soon to buy another is also ignored, and so is the surrender value of any life insurance policy or annuity, and up to 12 months arrears of mobility allowance, attendance allowance, income support, housing benefit or family credit. If you have more than £6,000, you will be expected to live off it (not squander it or give it away) until the amount you have is less than £6,000. If the DHSS thinks you have spent money faster in order to bring your capital below £6,000, they may treat you as though you still have it.

From September 1988 school-leavers under 18 will not be

able to claim income support – instead they will be expected to take up a place on the Youth Training Scheme. See p.127.

If you live with your husband or wife or other partner, either of you can claim income support, but you cannot both claim (and remember, you cannot claim if either of you is working for 24 hours or more per week). Both of your incomes will be taken into account, and if your joint income is below the income support level for a couple in your circumstances, the partner who made the claim will get the income support.

To claim income support, you must normally be available for work – meaning that you have to 'sign on' every two weeks. If you are working or studying part-time you must be available for a full-time job if one came up. The rules about availability for work are complicated, especially if you're studying – ask for help at your local Citizens Advice Bureau if you are unsure.

You can claim without having to sign on if you are a single parent, looking after a disabled or sick person, too ill or disabled to work, a woman who is due to have a baby within 11 weeks (or unable to work because of pregnancy) or if you are on an MSC, JTS or YTS scheme. You may also be able to claim if you are within 10 years of state retirement age (65 for men, 60 for women) and have not worked in the last 10 years and are unlikely to get work in the future.

How much?
There are four steps in working out how much income support you will get each week. The first three involve adding up the set amounts the government thinks you need to live on, and the fourth is subtracting the income you get each week. The amount of benefit you get is the difference between the two. However, if you were receiving supplementary benefit on 10 April 1988, your income support will not normally be less than the supplementary benefit you were receiving, plus a weekly amount (around £1.30) to help make up for the fact that with income support you have to pay 20 per cent of your rates (which were paid in full under the old system).

1 Personal allowances

These are the flat-rate amounts the government thinks you need for your day-to-day living expenses each week – food, clothes, fuel, laundry, travel, replacing household goods, television licence, etc. It is also expected to cover water rates and 20 per cent of your ordinary rates, but not other housing costs. What you get depends on your age and circumstances – for example, how many children you have. In 1988–89 the amounts are:

For a single person aged:
16 – 17	£19.40
18 – 24	£26.05
25 or over	£33.40

For a single parent aged:
16 – 17	£19.40
18 or over	£33.40

For a couple aged:
both under 18	£38.80
18 or over (one or both)	£51.45

For each child aged:
under 11	£10.75
11 – 15	£16.10
16 – 17	£19.40
18 or over	£26.05

(To get an addition for a child aged 16 or over, he or she must be studying full-time, at 'A' level or Ordinary National Diploma standard or below.)

2 Premiums

These are extra weekly amounts of benefit for people in certain categories. If you qualify for more than one premium you normally get whichever is the higher, but in some cases you can get both.

There are three premiums involving children: the family premium, the disabled child's premium and the lone parent premium. A single premium of £6.15 per week is paid as family premium if you have one or more children. Only one premium is payable, however many children you have. It is paid *in addition* to any other premium you are entitled to. The disabled child's premium is a premium of £6.15 per week for *each* child who is registered blind, or getting attendance or mobility allowance. It is paid in addition to any other premium you are entitled to. The lone parent premium is a single premium of £3.70 per week if you're bringing up one or more children on your own. Only one premium is payable, however many children you have. It is paid in addition to family premium and disabled child premium. If you're entitled to any other premiums you'll get whichever is higher.

There are also premiums for sick or disabled people. The disability premium is payable if you or your partner have been incapable of work for at least 28 weeks (you must have been sending doctor's certificates), or if you are receiving attendance or mobility allowance, invalidity benefit or severe disablement allowance, or if you're registered blind or have an invalid carriage, car or private car allowance from the DHSS. The premium is £13.05 per week for a single person and £18.60 for a couple. Only one premium is payable even if both partners in a couple qualify. It is paid in addition to family, disabled child or severe disability premium.

You can get the severe disability premium if you receive attendance allowance and live alone and no-one is getting invalid care allowance (see p.115) for looking after you. You will be counted as living alone if the only people who live with you are dependents under 18, boarders or people who receive attendance allowance as well. The premium is £24.75 for each person who qualifies – a couple will get £49.50 if they both qualify. It is paid in addition to family premium, disabled child premium, and to either disability premium or higher pensioner premium (see below).

There are also premiums for people aged 60 or over.

3 Housing requirements
If you get income support, you will automatically get housing

benefit as well to cover 80 per cent of your rates, and all your rent if you're a tenant. Your personal allowance is supposed to cover your water rates, 20 per cent of your ordinary rates and any repairs and insurance. However, you can get extra income support to cover mortgage interest payments – though if you are under 60, you will only get half of your mortgage interest paid for the first 16 weeks of a new claim. If this reduction means that you don't qualify for income support (but you would if your mortgage interest was paid in full) you must still claim – otherwise you will never qualify. You cannot get income support to cover repayment of the capital borrowed on mortgage. If you have a repayment mortgage, you could ask the lender to let you pay interest only for a while.

You can also get extra to cover the interest on loans for home improvement and repairs, provided the DHSS consider the repairs or improvement essential. However, if you have savings over £500, you'll only get interest paid on the part of the loan which your remaining savings won't cover.

Income support may also cover ground rent or service charges for owner-occupiers.

You may not get the full amount of your housing costs if the DHSS considers they are unreasonably high, or if you have other people living with you who are not dependent on you (for example, a grown-up child or a lodger).

Your personal allowances, and any premiums and housing costs you are entitled to, are added up to give your total requirements – known as the 'applicable amount'. The final step is:

4 Deducting your income
Your income is taken to be:

● your average weekly earnings from a job or self-employment plus those of your partner (but not those of any child under 16). The figure to use is what is left per week after tax, National Insurance and half of any pension contributions have been deducted. You can also deduct £5 for each person working (£15 if you are a single parent or disabled – but you can only have one lot of £15 per couple). You cannot deduct anything for the costs of working, such as travel or childminding expenses, though if you are self-employed you can deduct essential expenses of the business such as loan interest.

- the average weekly amount of any pension or social security benefits (apart from mobility and attendance allowance, housing benefit, resettlement benefit and £5 of any war pension), maintenance payments, MSC or YTS training allowance, student grant or sick pay. Any educational maintenance grant (see p.121) or fostering allowance is ignored. Other types of income are counted in part – the rules can be quite complicated.
- 'assumed' income from any savings above £3,000 of £1 a week for every £250 of savings. Any actual income (such as building society interest) is added to the amount of the savings before calculating the amount of assumed income. The other circumstances when the DHSS may also assume you are receiving income are if you are on strike, doing unpaid voluntary work, or if you are owed money.

How benefit is paid

Income support is generally paid every two weeks in arrears. Your first payment will probably come by post, with a form which gives a brief breakdown of how it is worked out. If you want a more detailed explanation you can ask for one. In some cases, you may get an order book that can be cashed weekly. The benefit is tax-free unless you are unemployed or on strike.

You must tell the DHSS of any change in your circumstances, as it may mean that your entitlement to benefit may change immediately.

Additional benefits
If you qualify for income support you also get free prescriptions and dental treatment, NHS vouchers to help with the cost of glasses, free school meals for your children, free milk and vitamins for expectant and nursing mothers and children under 5, and refund of fares to hospital. You may also qualify for payments from the Social Fund for maternity and funeral expenses (provided you have less than £500 in savings), and for loans to help with exceptional expenses (see p.52).

How to claim
If you are unemployed, ask at the local unemployment benefit office for form B.1. Send it to the address you are given.

If you do not have to sign on as unemployed, claim on form SB.1, available from your post office, local social security office or CAB. You can then decide whether to fill in the form yourself (ask your CAB for help if you find this difficult) or have an interview at home or at the social security office.

However you claim, you will have to provide evidence of your income, savings, children and any other information needed (for example, the hours you work).

For more information on the income support scheme, see social security leaflet SB.20.

The Social Fund

The Social Fund is a completely new scheme for people who do not have enough money to meet certain expenses. It replaced the supplementary benefit single payments scheme from April 1988. Certain payments are made as grants, while others are repayable interest-free loans. Some are paid as of right while others are discretionary, made from a cash-limited budget.

Maternity payment
If you have a new baby and get income support or family credit you can get a single grant of £85, but you'll get £1 less

for each £1 of any savings you have over £500. See DHSS leaflet FB.8 *Babies and Benefits* for more details. Claim on form SF.100 between 11 weeks before and 3 months after the birth.

Community care grants

These are only made to people on income support, or coming out of residential care and likely to get income support. Grants can be made to help you set up home or to move or improve your existing home if this would help you avoid going into residential care – e.g. to cover moving costs and costs of furniture and clothing. You might also get a grant to help cope with difficult family problems such as long-term illness or marriage breakdown. Grants won't have to be repaid, but they are discretionary and come out of a limited budget – so there's no guarantee that you'll get anything. Ask for Form SF.300 to make a claim.

Budgeting loans

Budgeting loans are only made to people who have been on income support for 26 weeks or more, to help pay for items such as furniture or house repairs. They are discretionary, and whether you get one depends on what priority the DHSS thinks you are compared to other applicants, and how much money there is in the local budget. You cannot get a budgeting loan if you are on strike. You may be refused a loan if the social fund officer thinks you will have trouble paying it back. You may only receive advice on managing your money or be referred to a charity or voluntary organization for help. If a loan is made, the repayments will be stopped from your weekly benefit at a fixed rate, and you can't owe the fund more than £1,000. Claim on form SF.300.

Crisis loans

Crisis loans can be made to anyone to help them cope with an emergency or disaster (such as a burglary or a fire) if there is no other way of preventing a serious risk to health and safety. The loan is discretionary in the same way as a budgeting loan. If you are on income support, the repayments will be deducted from your weekly benefit – if not, you will have to agree how you will repay. You must contact your local social security office for an interview to claim a crisis loan.

Reviews and appeals
If you are refused a maternity expense payment you can appeal to an independent tribunal – ask for an appeal form and get help from your local CAB filling it in.

There is no right of appeal with any other social fund payment. If you are refused payment or disagree with any aspect of the decision you can only ask for the decision to be reviewed by the DHSS. If you disagree with the rate of repayment of a loan, you cannot get this reviewed, although there is a complaints system.

For more information on the Social Fund, see social security leaflet SB.16, *A Guide to the Social Fund*.

4 Separation and divorce

For people without children, separation can be a perfectly amicable decision to go their separate ways and an unemotional division of property. But for many people with children there will be problems over custody of the children and access to them, over the home and the division of the property, and over money. These aspects are likely to loom much larger than the legal side of a divorce.

Where the divorce is not defended (hardly any are), it is possible to handle the legal arrangements yourself with the help of a book or two. Of you can ask a solicitor to look after the legal side for you. In any event you are likely to need some help sorting out what is to happen to your children, your home and your money. It is well worth finding out if the divorce court in your area offers a free conciliation service which can help you come to a fair settlement without the expense and unpleasantness of a legal battle. Even with this help, you may still feel you need the advice of a solicitor on certain issues. You will certainly need one if your partner does not consent to a divorce, or if you want any type of injunction. Try to find a solicitor who specializes in family law and who operates the Legal Aid scheme. This is a scheme operated by solicitors which entitles people on lowish incomes to get free legal assistance and court costs paid. Some solicitors also operate a fixed-fee interview, under which you can have a half-hour discussion with the solicitor for £5. You may need a solicitor who is also willing to do emergency work. Most libraries and Citizens Advice Bureaux keep a list of solicitors in their region who operate Legal Aid, and this list also shows the types of legal work in which they specialize.

But you should not expect your solicitor to wage all-out war on your behalf and achieve miracles. There is only a certain amount of money to go round and, where there are children, the court will eventually have to approve that the division of property is fair and that the children are adequately provided for. Almost certainly you will all end up worse off than you were before the split, as there just will not be enough money to run two homes to the same standard as one. If you or your partner run up large legal bills (a solicitor's time is expensive, so this can happen very quickly), there will be less for everyone. So do realize (and try to get your partner to realize) that it is much more sensible if you can settle as much of the future as possible between you, rather than squabble over the past.

Living arrangements

As long as you are married, both husband and wife have a right to live in the family home, whether it is privately owned or rented, and whether it is in one name or your joint names. But you may find it impossible to continue living under the same roof, or one may leave, or one may want the other to leave. You will no doubt also be concerned about what is to happen to the children (see next section) but we look first at the immediate problems which may arise.

A wife whose husband has been violent or has threatened violence towards her or the children can apply to the court for an order (called an injunction) which will enforce him to leave and not return. If she has been forced to leave her home, she can ask the court to make an order insisting that she and the children are allowed to return and live there. There are other types of injunction too, some of which can be obtained very quickly. You will find more information on them and what happens afterwards in a book called *Women's Rights* by Anna Coote and Tess Gill (Penguin). A solicitor's help will almost certainly be needed, and it's likely to cost £250 or more, though you can get Legal Aid if you qualify.

If your partner moves out of the home, and he or she was previously paying the mortgage payments (or rent) and the rates, you will need to make sure that these continue to be paid. If your partner is prepared to carry on paying them, ask the building society, council or whoever to tell you if any payments are missed, as not paying these essential bills could mean that you lose your home. If you find you have to pay them yourself and you are short of money there are various ways available for reducing the bills or getting them paid which are described later, or have been detailed in chapter 3.

If you own your home (as opposed to renting it), check whose name it is in. If you do not have any documents which show this, your solicitor or the organization which gave you the mortgage should be able to tell you. If it is in your partner's name alone, he or she has a right to sell it or get another mortgage on it without consulting you. You can prevent this happening by having the ownership transferred into your joint names, but this will take time and need your partner's co-operation. A much faster (and cheaper) way is to register a charge on the home (called a Class F Land Charge). You can ask a solicitor to do this for you (Legal Aid is available) but it is quite easy to do yourself. A Citizens Advice Bureau should be able to tell you exactly what to do. Your partner will not be told about your application, though once the charge is registered, he or she can find out if they ask. But your partner cannot then sell the home or use it as security for a loan without your consent.

If you leave home, you do not give up any of your rights to it but it may in practice make it harder to get it back. And it may not be at all easy to find somewhere else to live. If you cannot stay with friends or relatives, you can ask your local council to find you accommodation but it may be very poor and you may be told to apply for court injunctions so that you can return home. A woman in need of somewhere to live can go to a Women's Aid refuge – women can get the addresses from a Citizens Advice Bureau, Social Services department or the police.

If your home is rented and your partner has moved out, it would be sensible to tell the landlord about this and also who will be paying the rent in future.

Your children

While you are married, you each have rights and duties towards your children, such as the right to have your children live with you and to make decisions about them, and the duty to maintain them and see that they go to school. When you split up, these rights and duties will probably have to be split between you. One parent may have actual custody (often called care and control) of a child (i.e. the right to have the child living with him or her) while the other has access to the child. Sometimes both parents may have legal custody of the child – the right to make important decisions about him or her.

There are a number of circumstances in which you may want to apply to the court for actual custody of a child – for example if you cannot agree about who a child should live with, if your partner has the children and you think they would be better cared for with you, or if you are worried that your partner may try to take the children from you. Alternatively you can ask to have your child made a ward of court. Do not worry unduly at this stage if you cannot see how you can afford to support the child. You may well be entitled to social security benefits for yourself and the child. You can also apply for a court order to make your partner pay maintenance for a child in your care (see also p.65). You will need to discuss your circumstances in some detail with a solicitor so that he or she can advise you on what orders to apply for and in which court.

If you are getting divorced, the court must be satisfied about the arrangements for the children before the decree absolute can be granted. In deciding about care and control, access and custody, it will take into account the parents' and the child's wishes, the age and sex of the child, the child's general welfare and possibly the parents' conduct. It will want to be satisfied about where the children will live, about the arrangements that have been made about supporting them financially, about their education and about access to them, and will want to be satisfied that they receive proper care for any disabilities or long-term illnesses.

These arrangements can apply to any 'child of the family' under 18, including step-children and adopted children but not fostered children.

Money matters

Whether or not your separation is amicable, it is likely that money will become a bone of contention. People react in different ways: a partner with an income may refuse to contribute at all to the household budget; some people go on spending sprees or run up large bills in an attempt to forget their problems and cheer themselves up. Such action is understandable but only makes matters worse, especially for the partner left with the children.

Even if you think your partner has been spendthrift in the past and you could manage better on your own, it is most unlikely that you will end up better off after everything has been settled: separation is unlikely to change your partner's ways, and the same total amount of money is still going to have to support both of you and the children *and* pay for two homes *and* all the costs of the separation itself. So money is a vital issue.

Joint accounts
A joint bank, building society or credit card account can cause problems when you are splitting up. You could not stop your partner withdrawing all the money, or going on a spending spree which left a large overdraft. You might then find that you could be asked to repay money spent by your partner. A bank could even transfer money from your personal deposit or investment account to pay off what is owing on the joint account. So it is best to tell the bank or society what is happening as soon as you split up, close the joint account, agree on how much of the money in it each of you is going to get, and open individual accounts if you need them. At the very least you should write immediately to the bank or building society telling them only to accept cheques or withdrawals signed by both of you. You will also need to sort out who is going to pay the bills that have been paid by standing order or direct debit.

Not enough money
If you are short of money (perhaps because your partner is no longer supporting you or the children in your care) you can ask your local magistrate's court to make an order requiring your partner to make you regular payments (maintenance) or pay you a lump sum or both. If you are getting divorced or are legally separated, you can ask the Divorce Court to make such an order. You will be asked to provide details of all your income and expenditure and what you own. The court will also want to know about your partner's finances, and its decision may depend more on what your partner can afford than what you need. You may therefore find that you need to turn to social security benefits for help.

Even if you have agreed amicably that one of you will pay maintenance to the other or to the children, it is probably sensible for whoever has day-to-day responsibility for the children to insist that there is a court order covering the payments, so that they are legally enforceable.

Social security benefits

You may find that because of your reduced income you qualify for a number of social security benefits, particularly if you have dependent children. These benefits include family credit, income support, housing benefits (rent and rate rebates) and certain free health benefits. A separated wife may find she is entitled to unemployment benefit, even though she is not currently claiming it.

A man who is looking after children after separation becomes entitled to receive child benefit in place of the mother. He should apply to the local DHSS office for this. Any separated parent looking after a child or children can also claim one-parent benefit (£4.90 a week in 1988-89). Your children may qualify for free school meals and uniforms and educational maintenance allowances. More details of these benefits are given in chapter 9. If you have any difficulties claiming them, ask your Citizens Advice Bureau for help.

The tax situation

When you separate, the tax allowances you are each entitled to change. These allowances are not payments made to you; they are the amount of income you can have in a tax year without having to pay any tax on it. For the amounts, see chapter 3.

While you are married, the husband normally gets the married man's personal tax allowance which can be set against any of his or his wife's income. The wife gets the wife's earned income allowance which can only be set against the wife's earnings (but see p.35 for how these allowances are planned to change in 1990). After separation, you are both treated like single people again.

A man who separates from his wife will lose his married man's tax allowance at the end of the tax year (5 April). After that, he will get only a single person's tax allowance. If he has any children in his care, he can probably get the additional personal allowance as well, which makes his total personal allowances the same as the married man's allowance. He can also get some tax relief on any maintenance he pays to his separated or divorced wife (see p.66).

A wife with some income of her own gets favourable tax treatment in the tax year in which she separates from her husband. Her tax liability will be reduced and she may be due for a rebate. She should therefore tell her tax office (or the nearest one if she does not have one) the date on which she separated. The reason for the lower tax is the extra allowances she gets. She receives the wife's earned income allowance to set against what she has earned from the last 6 April up to the date of separation (her husband is liable for any tax on her investment income in this period). From the date of separation her income is treated separately from her husband's. She gets the single person's allowance to set against any of her income (from earnings or investments) from the date of separation until the next 5 April. And if she has any children living with her she can also get the additional personal allowance. This means she can have a total of £4,095 of income in this part of the year free of tax, and up to £6,700 in the whole tax year.

In each of the following tax years, a separated or divorced woman gets single person's allowance and, if she qualifies, the additional personal allowance and any other allowances she is entitled to. Any maintenance she gets from her former husband is now normally tax-free (see p.67).

Until the new system of taxing married couples is introduced in April 1990, while you are married and living together it is the husband who is responsible for declaring both incomes and paying all the tax (unless either of you has asked for separate assessment). From the date you separate permanently, you are each responsible for your own. This means it is up to each of you to claim any allowances you are entitled to, fill in any Tax Return you are sent and make sure that your PAYE code is correct.

Your home and possessions

While you are married, you each individually own the things that you bought, inherited or were given. But when you split up, the original ownership of things becomes less important. The first priority is to provide as well as possible for both parties, according to their needs and resources. It is best if you can agree with your partner as far as possible who is going to have what, and ask the court to approve what you have arranged. If you don't agree, the court can decide for you using the general guidelines given to it in law.

Rented homes
If the court decides that one of you is to stay in the home but the tenancy is not currently in that person's name, the court has the power to transfer the tenancy. If the lease says that the landlord's consent must be obtained to a transfer, it is sensible to ask for this in writing first, though the landlord cannot refuse unreasonably.

Owner-occupied homes
Your home may be in your joint names or one name alone, but this will have little influence on the court in deciding who is going to live in it or, if it is to be sold, how its value will be shared between you. The facts of your particular case are more important. Where there are children, the court must put their interests first and will try to ensure that whoever has care and control of them has a roof over their heads, at least until the children have finished their full-time education. So the parent who has care and control of all the children is likely to be allowed to stay on in the family home. But the other partner will want to get something for his or her share in the home.

There are four ways of arranging this, though each has its drawbacks and you need to examine the full repercussions of each. As an example, suppose a couple called Liz and David have two children and own a home worth £50,000 on which they have a mortgage of £30,000. Their own stake in the home is £20,000 and if they have lived together for several years and contributed in their different ways to providing for the family, this can be assumed to be £10,000 each. They are now getting divorced, and Liz has care and control of the children. The possibilities are:

Case 1

Liz stays in the home with the children, and it becomes her sole property. She buys David's £10,000 stake from him either by increasing the mortgage or by agreeing to get little or no maintenance for herself (David can still pay maintenance to support the children). This arrangement is fine for David but means that Liz's spendable income is cut back. If she increases the mortgage loan, she won't get any tax relief on the interest she pays on the extra mortgage, as she already owes £30,000 (the current ceiling for tax relief). She is likely to need help from social security.

Case 2

Liz stays in the home with the children until the youngest one finishes full-time education. David pays all or part of the mortgage repayments and helps support the children. The home is then sold and the mortgage paid off, and Liz and David share what is left. The main problem with this arrangement is that David gets nothing for his share in the home for a very long time, during which he is still having to pay the mortgage, so he is going to find it hard to pay for somewhere to live himself. A further snag is that he could lose the tax relief he gets on the mortgage and could find himself liable to capital gains tax when the house is sold. To avoid these possibilities it is important that David does not make the mortgage payments on the home he no longer lives in direct to the lender. He should make maintenance payments to Liz out of which she should pay the mortgage herself – the court order can include such an arrangement.

Case 3

They sell the home now, pay off the mortgage and split what is left. The problem for both Liz and David would be that, after paying all the costs involved, it is unlikely that they would have more than £9,000 each left. Unless they were each earning good money and living in areas with low house prices, they could not get large enough mortgages to buy new homes. However, if they had an £80,000 home and only a £30,000 mortgage, this option might be a good choice even if only David was working. If Liz were at home looking after the children she could perhaps have £40,000 of the £50,000 proceeds to buy a home outright. David could have the remaining £10,000 to put down as a deposit on a new home for himself, and raise a mortgage for the rest.

Case 4

David stays in the home and buys out Liz's £10,000 share by increasing the mortgage loan to £40,000. Liz could use this £10,000 as a deposit on a new home, as long as David paid her sufficient maintenance out of which to pay the mortgage. Liz would also need to find a lender who would give her a loan on the strength of her maintenance payments. But unless David's income were substantial, it is unlikely that he could afford all this. And as in Case 1, no tax relief would be available on the interest David paid on the extra £10,000 mortgage. Had the extra loan been within the £30,000 limit, it would be very important to ask a solicitor's advice on the wording of the divorce or separation agreement, to make sure that tax relief was obtained.

Which is the best solution for you will depend on the figures in your particular case. In your own long-term interest it would be worth doing the sums carefully. You will also need to take into account the effect of any maintenance which will be payable to your former partner and your children.

Your will

As your will says who you would like your possessions to go to on your death, it is very important to review it when you split up – or to make one if you have not done so. Solicitors generally charge around £30. If your income is low or you are on income support or family credit you may well qualify for free advice. Some of the more important points to consider are given in chapter 10.

Maintenance payments

When you separate, the parent who is left with the children or does not have a regular income is likely to need financial support from the other. The court will often make an interim order for maintenance soon after an application is made. When your separation looks set to be permanent, or before your divorce is finalized, it will make a permanent order. But these orders do not last forever. Maintenance to a former partner stops if either partner dies or if the recipient re-marries. Maintenance to children normally ends when the child reaches 17 or 18. And either payer or recipient can apply to the court at any time to change the amount of the payment if he or she thinks there is good reason. This means that if your partner cannot at present afford to pay you any maintenance, it is wise to get a court order for a nominal amount – 5 pence a year will do. Then if your partner's fortunes change, you can apply to the court to increase the amount (see p.69). This will be easier than trying to get a first order some years after the divorce.

In recent years there has been a tendency for husbands and wives to settle up by transferring lump sums of money rather than setting up orders for substantial maintenance payments, as it is likely to cause less resentment. There has also been a tendency to make maintenance payments to children rather than the ex-spouse, but this may change now that the tax situation has changed.

Maintenance payments and tax

The way in which maintenance payments are treated by the tax system was changed in the 1988 Budget. In the next section, 'new agreements' means ones which are dated on or after 15 March 1988. 'Old agreements' means legally binding ones which were dated before then and were sent to a tax inspector by 30 June 1988. But agreements which were in the pipeline during March-June 1988 can count as old agreements if a court order was applied for on or before 15 March 1988 and made by 30 June 1988, or if before 15 March 1988 you agreed on how much maintenance was to be paid, and you sent details to a tax inspector by 30 June 1988. A new agreement can also count as an old agreement if it replaces, varies or supplements an old agreement.

Tax relief for people who pay maintenance

Tax relief is only available on regular payments you make under a legally binding agreement such as a court order or separation deed. You cannot get tax relief on single lump sum payments, nor on any payments you make voluntarily.

Anyone making maintenance payments under a *new* agreement to his or her separated or divorced husband or wife can get tax relief on up to £1,490 of payments they make in each tax year (including the tax year in which the separation takes place). For example, if in the 1988–89 tax year you pay £100 a month (£1,200 over the year) in maintenance to your ex-wife, you will get tax relief on the full £1,200. So if you pay tax at the basic rate of 25%, you will escape paying tax on £1,200 of your income and save 25% of £1,200 which is £300. If you paid £150 a month (£1,800 over the year) you would get tax relief on £1,490, a tax saving of £372.50.

You can get tax relief on bills that a new agreement says you have to pay as well as on maintenance, but the amounts will count towards the £1,490 limit.

The £1,490 limit is likely to change each tax year, but will be equal to the difference between the single person's tax allowance and the married man's tax allowance for that tax year.

To claim your tax relief, send your tax inspector details of the court order or a copy of the maintenance agreement. If you are in a job and tax is deducted from your pay, you will get tax relief by getting a higher PAYE coding and less tax will be deducted from your wages. If you are self-employed your tax assessment will be reduced.

You cannot get tax relief on maintenance payments you make to your children under new agreements. And tax relief on payments to your ex-spouse will end if he or she re-marries.

If you make maintenance payments under an *old* agreement, you will continue to get tax relief in the same way as before, on the full amount of the payments. This includes payments to your children made under a UK court order, as well as payments to your separated or divorced husband or wife. But if the amount of the payments is increased at any time after 5 April 1989, you won't get tax relief on the extra. If you are in this situation and the amount you are allowed tax relief on is less than you would be allowed under a new agreement, you should ask for your old agreement to be treated as if it was a new one as from the beginning of the current tax year (or the previous tax year, if that would be beneficial).

If you or children in your care receive maintenance

Any maintenance payments you or your children get under a *new* agreement are tax-free. You don't have to pay any tax on them, however much other income you have.

If you receive maintenance payments under an *old* agreement from your separated or divorced husband or wife, the first £1,490 of what you get in the 1988–89 tax year is tax-free. The £1,490 limit is likely to change each tax year, but will be equal to the difference between the single person's tax allowance and the married man's tax allowance for that tax year.

If you get more than this under an old agreement, the rest will count as taxable income; tax will be payable on it if, when added to your other income, it comes to more than your total tax allowances for the tax year – but this will be unusual. If the amount of your maintenance payments is increased after 5 April 1989, the extra amount will always be tax-free.

Maintenance payments made to a child under an old agreement are taxable. But they count as the child's income (even if the money is actually paid to a parent) and it will normally be the case that the amount of maintenance the child receives each year is less than the child's own single person's tax allowance, in which case no tax will be payable on the maintenance payments themselves.

In some cases, maintenance paid under old agreements has basic rate tax already deducted from it by the payer. If the tax deducted is more than you are liable to pay, you can reclaim the extra from the Inland Revenue. After 5 April 1989, you should receive the full amount from the payer, with no tax deducted.

Problems with maintenance payments

Late payments

If your maintenance payments are falling behind, it is worth getting the maintenance order registered in the magistrate's court. The payer must then make the payments to the court, which will pass them on to you. This not only ensures that a record of the payments made is kept, but if they get behind you can ask the court to enforce them. If you want to do this, apply initially to the original divorce court. If the payer has disappeared, the DHSS may be able to trace him or her through his or her National Insurance number and tell the court where they are (but they won't tell you).

If payments are not being made regularly under an order registered in the magistrate's court, you can assign your payments over to the DHSS and get income support instead. This will at least mean you get your income regularly. The DHSS will then try to get the money out of the payer, but only up to the amount of benefit they pay you. If the amount of maintenance you are due is more than the amount of income support you get, you will have to chase the payer for the rest yourself.

Another way of getting someone who is in a job and is more than four weeks late in paying maintenance is to apply to the court for an 'attachment of earnings' order. The payer's employer will then have to deduct the payments from his or her pay and send them to the court who will send them on to you. The amount deducted can be both the regular amount and instalments of what is owing from the past. Of course, this method cannot be used if the payer is unemployed or self-employed.

There are other ways of enforcing maintenance payments, for which you will almost certainly need a solicitor's help. This may be expensive, so check that you can get Legal Aid or it may not be worth it.

Getting more maintenance

If you are finding it hard to manage on the maintenance payments you and your children get and you think your ex-husband or wife could pay more, you can go back to the court at any time and ask for the amount to be increased. If the order was registered in a magistrate's court, you should apply to the one where the registration was made, but if you have moved away, say, you can ask to have the case transferred locally. The court will want up-to-date details of your financial position and your reasons for the application. Of course, the person paying maintenance is equally entitled to ask the court at any time for a reduction in the amount payable – for example, if they find out that you are living with another person as a couple.

5 Single parents and unmarried couples

All of the information in chapter 3 – apart from the section on married couples only – applies equally to one-parent families and to parents who are not married. In some cases, as discussed there, one-parent families get preferential treatment (for example, single parents do not have to be available for work to qualify for income support). However, there are other factors which only concern lone parents – that is anyone who is single, widowed, separated or divorced who lives alone with their children. And in 1988–89 there are also special considerations for unmarried couples who live together with their children.

For lone parents

One-parent benefit
If you are bringing up any children on your own, you can probably get one-parent benefit as well as child benefit. This is a tax-free payment of £4.90 a week (the amount is the same, however many children you have).

You must normally be single, widowed, divorced or legally separated to qualify. If you are married, you can claim if you have been living apart for 13 weeks or more and the separation is likely to be permanent. You must not be living with anyone as husband and wife, and you must be getting child benefit for at least one child who lives with you (the child does not have to be your own). But you cannot get one-parent benefit if you get child's special allowance, guardian's allowance or certain other benefits for a child. Any income support, housing benefit, unemployment benefit or sickness benefit may be reduced by the amount of your one-parent benefit.

For more details, see DHSS leaflet CH.11 which has the claim form CH.11A attached to it. If you could have claimed one-parent benefit in the past but did not do so, your claim can be back-dated for up to a year.

If you get one-parent benefit, you can at any time choose to have both this and all your child benefit paid weekly instead of four-weekly. This is well worth doing as you will get the money up to four weeks earlier – which helps with budgeting.

The additional personal tax allowance

Lone and unmarried parents can claim an 'additional personal allowance' – that is an additional amount of income you can have in the tax year without paying any tax on it. As well as getting the normal single person's allowance (see p.34) the additional personal allowance lets you have a further £1,490 of income free of tax, a total of £4,095.

To get the allowance, you must have a child living with you for all or part of the tax year (from 6 April one year to 5 April the next). The child must be your own child, your step-child, a child you have legally adopted or any other child under 18 whose upkeep you pay for. If the child is over 16 at the start of the tax year, he or she must be in full-time education or on a full-time training course lasting at least two years.

Only one person can claim the full allowance in respect of one child, so if the child is living with another adult when he or she is not living with you, then either one of you (but not both) can claim the allowance, or it can be split between you.

A woman can get the additional person allowance in the tax year in which she separates from her husband or in which she is widowed, but a man cannot (but he does not lose his married man's allowance). If separated, each partner can get the additional personal allowance in future years if each has at least one child living with them.

You claim the additional personal allowance by filling in details of the child on your tax return, if you are sent one. If you are not, then write to your tax office explaining why you think you are entitled to the allowance.

Affiliation orders

A parent who is divorced or separated from his or her spouse can claim maintenance (see p.65), but if you are a single parent, you cannot claim maintenance for yourself from your former partner. An unmarried mother can, however, apply to the magistrate's court for an affiliation order to make the father of her children pay maintenance for them. She too can do this while she is pregnant or before the child's third birthday or later if she can show that she lived with the father or he paid money towards the child's upkeep in its first three years, but not if she and another man are living together as a couple. As well as regular maintenance payments, the court may order a lump sum of up to £500 to cover things like the cost of items needed for a new baby.

If the father is prepared to pay without a court order, the mother can get a form from the National Council for One-Parent Families for drawing up a legally enforceable agreement between them. If not, she will probably need a solicitor to help her apply through the court (she may be able to get Legal Aid for this). She will have to satisfy the court that the man she names is the father of the child in question.

Child's special allowance

Until 6 April 1987, a mother who was divorced or whose marriage was annulled and whose ex-husband died was entitled to child's special allowance, a tax-free payment of £8.05 a week for each child who lived with her or whom she helped to support. This allowance has now been abolished, but continues to be paid if you were getting it on 5 April 1987 – though you cannot get one-parent benefit as well as child's special allowance. The allowance will be paid for as long as you get child benefit for the child or until you remarry or live with a man as his wife.

If you are widowed

If you are a man whose wife dies, the only State benefit you might get directly is a payment from the social fund towards the cost of the funeral. If you have children, however, you will become entitled to the same benefits as other lone parents described in this chapter. You will receive child benefit, one-parent benefit and the same special tax allowances. If you stay at home to look after children you will get home responsibilities protection to protect your state basic pension (see p.37), and if your income is low you can claim the benefits described in chapter 3.

A woman who loses her husband is generally entitled to rather more because she will normally get widow's benefits from the State (provided her husband's National Insurance contribution record was sufficient). She may also get more generous treatment from her husband's employer's pension scheme, more life insurance benefits and more favourable tax treatment in the tax year in which her husband dies and the following one.

What a widow gets from the State depends on her age and whether she has any dependent children. A woman who is under 60 when her husband dies will normally get a tax-free lump sum widow's payment (£1,000 in 1988–89). If you have dependent children (or you're pregnant) you can get widowed mother's allowance of up to £41.15 per week (which is taxable) plus £8.40 tax-free for each dependent child. You may get a reduced amount, depending on your husband's National

Insurance contribution record. A woman aged 45 or over when her husband dies or when her entitlement to widowed mother's allowance ends can claim widow's pension. The amount will depend on your husband's National Insurance record, but the maximum per week is £41.15 if you're aged 55 or over when you qualify, reduced by 7 per cent (£2.88) for each year you're aged under 55. You'll lose entitlement to widowed mother's allowance or widow's pension if you remarry or while you live with a man.

See the leaflet NP.45 *A Guide to Widow's Benefits* for more details, and use form BW.1 from your local DHSS office to claim any widow's benefit.

Unmarried couples

The additional personal allowance

At present, living together does not affect your entitlement to the additional personal allowance. If you have a child who meets the conditions on page 38, either you or your partner can claim this tax allowance or you can agree to split it between you. Generally it will be best if whoever has the higher income claims it.

If you have more than one child, you can each claim the additional personal allowance in respect of a child who meets the conditions. For example, if you have a child and your partner has one of his or her own, you can each claim the allowance for your own child. If you have no children but your partner has two or more and you arrange your finances so that you maintain one of these children, you can claim for that child and your partner can claim for one of the others.

At the present time, therefore, you can each have a single person's allowance and the additional personal allowance. In the 1988–89 tax year this means you can each have £2,605 + £1,490 = £4,095 of income free of tax, a total of £8,190 before you start paying tax. This is a substantial benefit over a married couple, who can only have a maximum of £6,700 free of tax.

But from 6 April 1989 the rules are to change so that an unmarried couple who live together as husband and wife will not be able to claim more than one additional personal allowance between them. They will therefore get the same total allowances as a married couple.

Mortgages on a shared home

The tax relief available when two or more people who are not married to each other have either a joint mortgage or separate mortgages on a single property is due to change on 1 August 1988.

For loans taken out before that date, each person can get tax relief on the interest he or she pays on up to £30,000 of loans. So two single people who share a home which they have bought in their joint names can get tax relief on a total of £60,000 of loans, twice as much as a married couple. To get the full benefit of this, try to arrange things so that, before either partner pays interest on an amount over £30,000, the other is paying interest on a full £30,000, as otherwise you would lose some relief. For example, if one of you were paying the interest on £20,000 and the other on £40,000, the first would get tax relief on £20,000 but the second only on £30,000. But if each paid the interest on £30,000, each would get relief on the whole of the interest they paid.

Loans taken out before 1 August 1988 will continue to be treated in this way for the life of the loan. Even if the loan is actually made on or after 1 August 1988, it will be treated as above if, before that date, you have exchanged contracts to buy the home and have got a written mortgage offer.

With this exception, loans made on or after 1 August 1988 will be treated differently. The £30,000 limit will apply to all the loans on a single property, and will be divided equally between each 'sharer'. So if two people each have a loan (or share a joint loan) on their shared home, each can get tax relief on the interest they pay on up to £15,000 – called the 'sharer's limit'. But if one sharer pays interest on less than their sharer's limit, they can transfer the unused part to another sharer. For example, if Mark pays interest on £10,000 and Sue on £30,000, Mark can transfer his unused £5,000 to Sue so that Sue can get tax relief on her own £15,000 limit plus the transferred £5,000, in other words on £20,000.

Covenant payments
Before the 1988 Budget it was possible for unmarried couples to save a lot of tax if one had a low income, by the other making a deed of covenant to the low earner. You could also make deeds of covenant to your partner's children even if they lived with you, as long as they were not your own children. The effect was that the payer got tax relief on the amount paid over, and the recipient would not have to pay tax on it if his or her income, including the covenanted payments, came to less than his or her personal tax allowances.

Tax relief will continue to apply to existing covenants which were made before 15 March 1988 and sent to a tax inspector by 30 June 1988. But it is no longer possible to get tax relief on new covenants, as they are ignored by the tax system: the payer does not get any relief on what he pays, while for the recipient the money he gets is tax-free.

6 While you are at work

A major problem facing all parents when the one who has been looking after the children wants to return to work is that of what to do with them during the day.

Compared with many other countries, nursery provision in Britain is very poor. Although the law now gives working mothers the right to return to their jobs within 29 weeks of the birth of their baby, this right is of little use if you cannot find anywhere for your child to be well looked after while you are at work, or if such facilities are so expensive that you cannot afford to use them.

This may mean you have to depend on your family, relatives, friends or neighbours to look after your baby or young child at times. In some families a grandparent who lives nearby is the answer. There is, in fact, no law as such against leaving a child alone, or with older children or other adults; the law only states that you (and anyone over 16 looking after the child) must not neglect the child or expose it to any unnecessary suffering.

The other alternatives are to make private child care arrangements, to use a registered childminder – details of those in your area can be obtained from the social services department of your local council – or a nursery school – information about local authority ones will be at the council's education department. Not all these may be available in the area where you live.

Facilities provided by your employer

Your employer can help you in two ways – either by paying some or all of the cost of placing your child in a private nursery, or by providing nursery facilities at your workplace for any employees to use. Neither of these provisions is compulsory, and only a small minority of companies provide either of them.

Where the employer contributes towards the cost of a private nursery, he is likely only to offer a particular one with which the firm has a special arrangement. This may be neither the cheapest nor the best in the area, and your firm may have only a set number of reserved places, so that if all these are taken you may have to make other arrangements. If your employer pays his contribution to the nursery direct, you will not normally be charged any tax on the benefit you get from using the nursery unless your earnings in the tax year (plus the amount your employer pays the nursery) come to more than £8,500. But if your employer gives you the money to pay the nursery yourself, or adds it to your wages or gives you any sort of voucher you can use in part payment, the amount you get will be taxable (provided that your earnings, including this contribution, are high enough for you to pay tax).

If your employer provides a nursery on the premises, you may again have the problem of there being a fixed number of places. The employer can charge you for using it, though the firm will usually meet part of the cost. There will be no tax to pay on the benefit you get from using these facilities unless, as with the payment to an outside nursery, the amount it costs your employer to provide the place for your child when added to your pay over the tax year comes to more than £8,500. In this case you will be taxed on the whole cost of the nursery provision. For example if you earn £8,200 and it costs your employer £500 a year to provide the facilities for your child, you will be taxed on the £500 as well as your wages. (Of course, it is still preferable to pay the £125 tax due than pay the nursery costs of £500.)

How suitable a nursery at or near your work is much depends on how easy and how long your journey to work is. Five minutes walk with a two-year-old is clearly preferable to over an hour by train and bus. Another consideration is that if you lose your job or want to change it or need to move home you will lose the nursery facility as well. However, you may consider it an advantage to have the child near at hand.

Other child care facilities

Nursery schools

Nursery schools are not specifically provided for looking after children while parents are at work, but are intended rather as a part-time introduction to school. In most parts of the country there are very few local authority nursery schools (or nursery classes attached to primary schools) and so they do not take many children before they are three or four. Putting your child's name on a waiting list as far ahead as possible – while still a baby if possible – will certainly help.

Although nursery schools run by the local authority are free and should provide good care and facilities for your child, they are often not much help if both parents want to work full time. Even if they will take two-year-olds, they won't normally take children younger than that. Their hours are normally no longer than 9.30 to 3.30 and it is common for children to be restricted to the morning or afternoon sessions only. In addition, many schools are open only during normal term times and are closed during school holidays.

There may be one or more private nursery schools in your area, and these may be able to take children for something like a full working day, but you will of course have to pay. The cost is likely to be around £250 to £400 per term for a child attending five days a week, £150 to £250 for a child attending each morning. Many schools charge more for babies than toddlers.

These schools have to be registered with the local council which will check up on the facilities and safety aspects from time to time, but the staff do not have to be qualified teachers or nursery nurses, nor is there any check on the educational standards. This does not mean that the schools will not be very good: you can find out about them by asking around, and by visiting them.

Day nurseries

The Social Services departments of local councils run day nurseries which may be able to take children for longer hours than most nursery schools (for example, from 8am to 6pm). This makes them much more suitable for children of parents who want or need to work full-time. However, how likely you are to get a place for your child depends on how much you are thought to need it. In practice, this means that your child is unlikely to get a place unless you are a single parent, or the parent who normally looks after the children cannot do so because of illness, or you live in poor housing conditions.

Local authority day nurseries may be very cheap or even free to people who live in the area. How much you have to pay often depends on your income and circumstances – for example £25 for a 5-day week if you are on a reasonable wage, £1 a week if you are out of work. You cannot claim any tax relief on what you have to pay. The premises and equipment vary a lot in different areas, but they are normally staffed partly by trained nursery nurses.

There may also be some private day nurseries in your area, open most days of the year and able to take children from around 8.30am to 6pm. In other respects they are much like private nursery schools, but may cost more because of the longer day and greater number of staff required – £30 to £60 a week is fairly common.

Childminders
A childminder is someone who looks after other people's children in their own home as a way of earning money. They are most likely to charge something between £15 and £30 for looking after a baby or young child for a full five-day week. A childminder who has children for more than two hours a day must be registered with the social services department of the local council, who can give you a list of registered childminders in your area. The local council check that the home is safe and kept clean and will set the maximum number of children the minder may accept. But many childminders are not registered so that they can take more children than the council would let them – at the risk of being taken to court and fined. It is worth checking that the childminder you are considering is registered, though this does not tell you anything about how good the person is with children. You can get more information about childminders from the National Childminding Association (13 London Road, Bromley, Kent, BR1 1DE).

Playgroups
Most playgroups are run by a group of mothers who may employ one person to take responsibility for organizing the sessions but the mothers themselves normally help supervise on a rota basis. Many playgroups are only open in the mornings and not always every morning, so they may not be much help to a parent who wants to work full-time. They are, however, cheap to use – around £1 a morning is typical – and there is not usually much problem about getting your child into a playgroup, as long as you are prepared to help out when it is your turn. Some groups have a higher charge if you are unable to help occasionally.

Playgroups are often held in hired premises like church halls which may limit the number of toys and equipment they can have. The emphasis is on play and social development rather than pre-school education, though some groups include some basic reading, writing and counting as well as singing and structured games. They do not normally take children under two and a half or three, and in some areas it is usual for children to go on to a nursery class when they are four.

Playgroups must be registered with the Social Services department of the local council who check up on safety, accommodation and the facilities provided. The council may give them some financial support, and may run courses for people who want to train as playgroup leaders. You can get more information from the Pre-School Playgroups Association, Alford House, Aveline Street, London SE11. Most playgroups are affiliated to this association.

Providing services yourself

The difficulty of finding suitable care for your child during the working day may encourage or enforce you to set up your own nursery. If you choose to do this, you could work in conjunction with other parents who would form a committee to run the nursery and employ professional people (such as trained nursery nurses) to run it. You can get a leaflet *Self-help Day Care Schemes* which explains what is involved from Gingerbread (the Association for One-Parent Families, 35 Wellington Street, London WC2E 7BN).

Alternatively, you could consider running a nursery yourself as a money-earning proposition, or being a childminder. In either case, contact the local authority Social Services department to talk it over first. They can explain their requirements and what you will need to provide to qualify for registration. They may also know of a short course you can attend.

To be accepted as a childminder, you will have to have adequate facilities at your home and may need to buy cots, small chairs and tables, a playpen and toys. The National Childminding Association (address above) will also be able to send you information, supply standard agreements and arrange public liability insurance for you. You will count as self-employed, and should contact the DHSS and your tax office to tell them what you are up to.

Employing your own help

A further alternative for child care is to employ someone to look after your children in your own home. This could be someone who lives locally and comes in when required, or you could have a nanny or au pair living in. When you taken on someone in this way, you may be acting as an employer, and this role may carry with it certain rights and duties and financial complications. These are dealt with below.

Nannies

If you don't have a specific person in mind, you could look for people advertising themselves as available for this kind of work in local newspapers and shops. It is also worth asking at your local Jobcentre – they may well know of someone looking for this type of work. There may be self-employed people in your area who will come to your home at the same times each week to look after your children. If you are wanting someone to live in you could look in places such as *The Lady* magazine. This also carries advertisements for nanny agencies you could contact, and you can also advertise the job yourself, of course.

You may decide you want someone with previous experience or who can give you references or who is a trained nursery nurse with an NNEB (National Nursery Examining Board) certificate. You can expect a nanny to take complete responsibility for your children during her working hours, seeing to their meals, playing with them, teaching them, dressing them and so on. If she were working for 40 to 45 hours a week you could expect to pay her between £40 and £60 a week if she lives in and between £50 and £100 if she comes in daily and is provided with meals while at your home. You can check the current rates from other advertisements and information produced by the agencies. You may be able to reduce the cost by sharing your nanny with another family, so that she looks after your children and theirs at the same time, perhaps in your house on some days and in theirs on others.

Before advertising for anyone or interviewing them, it is sensible to decide in some detail how many hours a week you want the nanny to work, exactly what you want her to do, whether you want her to live in your home, when you want her to start and how much you can afford to pay. If you are going to have to pay employer's National Insurance contributions to the DHSS on top of the wages you pay (see below), you need to allow for this.

Employing someone in the home

The financial relationship between you and someone who works for you depends on the circumstances. It is important to get it sorted out with the tax office and the DHSS early on, or you could land yourself with problems. In some circumstances you have to deduct tax and National Insurance contributions from your nanny's pay. If you fail to do so it is probable that you will be liable for paying them, not the nanny. The rules can be complex and the guidance here is only general, so do get advice from the authorities.

If your nanny comes through an agency and you pay the agency each week or month and the agency pays her wages, she will probably count as the agency's employee. The agency will be liable for deducting any tax and National Insurance due from what it pays her. There is nothing for you to do apart from pay the agency.

If your nanny regularly works for the other people as well as yourself, advertises her services, states her charges and does not live in, she probably counts as self-employed and all you need to do is to pay her the rates you have agreed. She will be liable to pay her own tax and National Insurance contributions.

If your nanny works for you for only a few hours a week for a small wage, the arrangement between you can be very informal and no authorities need be involved. She should inform the tax office about her earnings, but it is unlikely that you will be asked to take any action.

Above certain limits, however, a more formal relationship is established, there are duties and procedures you must perform and the employee acquires rights you must respect. If you employ someone (who does not count as self-employed) for more than 16 hours a week, she will acquire rights under the employment laws after two years. Even if you employ someone for only eight or more hours a week, she will acquire the same rights after five years. For example, with each pay packet you must give her a piece of paper which shows what you have paid her and how much tax, National Insurance and anything else you have deducted from her wages. After a month she has the right to be given a minimum period of notice, and within 13 weeks you must give her a written contract of employment. After two years the employee becomes entitled to the right to claim unfair dismissal, and a set payment if you make her redundant (though people over pension age do not get all these rights). There is more information in the booklet *Individual Rights of Employees* and other Department of Employment leaflets which you can obtain free at any Jobcentre.

If you pay your nanny more than the current National Insurance lower earnings limit (£41 a week in 1988–89), you will have to deduct her National Insurance contributions from her pay and pay employer's National Insurance contributions yourself. (It is not worth paying someone a pound or two more than the lower earnings limit, because she will actually end up with less money in her pocket than if you paid her wages of just less than the limit.) You may also have to deduct income tax under the PAYE system. As soon as you have appointed someone on a wage higher than the lower earnings limit (or as soon as you have agreed to increase an existing employee's wages above this level) you should tell your local DHSS office and also your tax office. You will be sent deduction cards on which you have to record how much you have paid the person each week or month, and how much tax and National Insurance you have deducted (you get sets of tables for working these out), and you have to pay them to the Collector of Taxes every three months. If your nanny is off work through illness for more than three days you may have to pay her Statutory Sick Pay for up to 28 weeks, but you can deduct what you pay from the National Insurance contributions and tax you send to the tax collector. Each April you have to send in the deduction cards and an employer's declaration. You will be sent leaflets explaining all these procedures, but if you want to see what is involved in advance, ask at your social security office for NP.15 *Employer's Guide to National Insurance Contributions* and NI.227 *Employer's Guide to Statutory Sick Pay* and at your tax office for P.7 *Employer's Guide to PAYE*.

Au pairs

An au pair is a girl of 17 or above, normally from another country, who lives as a member of your family. In return for helping around the home and with the children, you provide her with accommodation and pay her at least £20 a week, and normally between £25 and £35. She is not a full-time nanny, and cannot normally be expected to work or look after children for more than five hours a day. She must be given a fair amount of free time including one whole day and three or four evenings each week to study, attend courses or whatever.

An au pair may not have any experience of or qualifications for looking after children, and if you want her to do so you should make it clear at the outset. There are agencies which match families to au pairs and some of these advertise in *The Lady* magazine, though they may charge £100 or more for finding you someone. There are conditions about employing au pairs from abroad which you must comply with; you can find out about these from the Home Office or the agency.

7 Children's income and savings

As children get older there are various ways they can get their own money, and ways to save it.

Pocket money

Pocket money is generally seen as a useful way of teaching children to manage their own resources and make their own spending and saving decisions. Many parents give their children a small amount of money regularly each week for saving or spending. Around the age of five or six this is generally for treats, toys, books or whatever. As the children get older the amount of money normally gets larger, but this may be on condition that the children buy some of the necessities of life for themselves, perhaps paying their own fares, as well as luxuries. Part of the money may be earmarked for particular purposes, such as for saving or for a clothing allowance. Some parents also tie what they pay to the amount of help that children give around the home, so that part or all of the money is earned rather than given.

Each year, Wall's Ice Cream carry out a survey of how much pocket money children of different ages get. The averages in early 1988 were:

5–7 years:	54p a week
8–10 years:	95p a week
11–13 years:	£1.47 a week
14–16 years:	£2.12 a week

However much you give your children, there is no tax to be paid by them on it. On the other hand, you cannot claim that because you have given the money away it should no longer count as your taxable income. Nor are you going to be liable for inheritance tax on what you have given away, because regular gifts of money made out of your income and gifts for the maintenance or education of your children are exempt from this tax.

Children's earnings

Jobs at home

As a parent, you do not have a legal right to insist that your children do jobs around the home, though you may of course consider it an essential part of their upbringing that they do so. Whether or not you give them any payment for domestic chores is entirely up to you: while some parents feel that payment for jobs gives children an incentive and encourages them to make their own decisions, others feel that it is wrong to commercialize relationships within the family and that children should help out for reasons of consideration for other people rather than for money.

Some families have a very informal system of payment, whereby the children get money occasionally when the parents feel they have been especially helpful. Other families have quite rigorous systems, whereby different jobs each earn so much money or so many points towards a weekly total. These jobs may include cleaning the home, making beds, washing up, cleaning shoes, ironing, shopping, cooking, gardening, mowing, cleaning the car, looking after younger brothers and sisters, exercising the dog and helping with decorating.

Employment

Children under 13 are not allowed to work by law, unless the local authority has made bye-laws which allow certain kinds of work. Common exemptions are being allowed to work for up to one hour before school (doing a paper round, for example), or to help with light work on a farm they live on.

There are special rules for children employed in the entertainments industry. Basically, the employer must obtain a licence from the local authority if a child under 16 is taking part in a public performance, film, television programme, etc. A licence is not needed for purely amateur productions.

Between 13 and the official school-leaving age, children are not supposed to work during school hours, nor before 7am or after 7pm, nor for more than two hours on a school day or a Sunday. There are also restrictions on the places they can work (no factories, construction sites, mines or quarries) and on the type of work they can do (no lifting things which are heavy enough to cause injury).

There are also a number of restrictions on the work that can be done by young people who have left school but are still under 18. These apply to particular types of work, like not doing night work and not working for more than a certain number of hours in a day or a week in industry. However, employers may be able to get permission to ignore these restrictions.

One of the most common ways for children to earn a few pounds a week is by delivering newspapers. Shops which employ children on paper rounds are vetted by the local authority, and the hours that children are allowed to work are governed by local bye-laws. Large numbers of teenage children also work in shops on Saturdays and after school.

If a child of yours is earning money, you have no legal right to insist that they use some of it to pay some of the cost of their upkeep. But once a child is 18, there is no longer any obligation on you to support them.

Odd jobs and small businesses

Many older children do baby sitting, grass cutting, car washing, dog walking and so on for people in their neighbourhood, to earn some extra money. The cheapest way for them to advertise such services is to make some photocopied leaflets saying how much they charge and giving the name and phone number, and deliver these to local houses, or to put a postcard in a local shop window. Once they get known, word of mouth is usually sufficient on its own. Parents may need to keep quite a close watch on what children are actually doing, particularly if dangerous equipment like lawn mowers is involved.

Your child may be talented enough to start providing a more specialized or professional service or to make or buy items which they are able to sell at a reasonable profit. Occasionally these ventures are very successful and can produce quite a high income. If your child has a turnover of a few hundred pounds a year, you should make sure that they are keeping accurate records of all their costs and all their income as they may have to show these to the Inland Revenue or the Customs and Excise. If the business is taking up a lot of the child's time, you will have to decide whether school work is suffering as a result, and which you think is the more important.

You should make sure that your child's venture is within the law (for example, children under 17 must not be street traders) and conforms to local bye-laws. You can ask the local education welfare officer about this (contact the education department of your local authority).

Tax and National Insurance

It is commonly believed that under a certain age children do not have to pay tax, but this is not the case. The reason that most children do not pay tax is simply that their taxable income is not high enough. From the time of birth a child counts as a single person for tax purposes. This means that if the child's 'taxable income' in a tax year is more than their tax allowances, they have to pay tax on the difference. Each child gets a single person's tax allowance, so that each child can have taxable income of up to that amount each year (£2,605 in the 1988–89 tax year) without being liable to any income tax. If your child's income were more than this, the child would be liable for tax on the difference. For example, if in 1988–89 a child's taxable income was £2,800, tax would be charged on £195 (i.e. £2,800 less £2,605) and tax on this at the basic rate of 25% would be £48.75 (i.e. £195 × 0.25).

'Taxable income' means earnings from an employment, profits on a business and any money taken out of the business, and interest on certain investments (for example, company share dividends, National Savings investment account, interest payments on British Government stock). It also includes money paid to the child under a deed of covenant made (or agreed) before 15 March 1988 and maintenance payments payable to the child under a court order made (or agreed) before 15 March 1988 (but not payments *for* the child). Where tax has been deducted from any of this income before the child received it, the amount of tax deducted must also be included in the 'taxable income'. (This would include tax credits and tax vouchers attached to share and unit trust dividend payments.)

'Taxable income' does not include prizes, gifts, presents, pocket money, grants and scholarships for education, interest credited to a bank or building society savings or deposit account (unless the child's income is very high), interest on National Savings Certificates, the first £70 of interest credited to a National Savings ordinary account, nor increases to social security benefits paid for children. Nor does it include payments under most maintenance or covenant agreements made on or after 15 March 1988.

There is no qualification to this. If parents invest money in their child's name, or if they give a child of theirs money which the child invests, any interest or other income the child gets from the investments is taxed as though it was the parents' income, not the child's. 'Child' here means a child who is under 18 and unmarried. The reason for this rule is to stop parents avoiding tax by simply putting their investments in their children's names. However, there are two exceptions to this rule. If the child's income from these sources is less than £5 in the tax year, the income is treated as the child's. And income earned by an accumulation trust of which your child is the beneficiary is not taxed as yours if it is accumulated in the trust, only if it is paid out (see p.106).

If a child gets any income from which tax has already been deducted (such as dividends on company shares or unit trusts and certain covenant and maintenance payments), this tax can be reclaimed from a tax office if the child's taxable income in the tax year (including the tax deducted) is less than the personal allowance. In practice, the parents may reclaim this tax on the child's behalf.

Tax can also be reclaimed if the amount deducted from the child's income is more than the child should have paid. To check this:

- add up all the income your child has received in the tax year which is included in the definition of 'taxable income' above, remembering to include the amounts of any tax deducted
- from this subtract the outgoings and allowances the child can claim. In the vast majority of cases this will only be the single person's allowance, but you can check using the notes which accompany a Tax Return or with an up-to-date income tax guide
- if you are left with a minus number your child should not have paid any tax and you can claim any which has been deducted from income in the 'taxable income' list above
- if you are left with a positive number, multiply it by the basic rate of tax (remembering to divide by 100 as it is a percentage) to find out how much tax the child should have paid. If more than this amount has been deducted from income in the 'taxable income' list above, you can reclaim the difference. If less has been deducted, you or your child will probably be asked to hand over the difference.

To reclaim tax, ask your tax office either for a Tax Return for your child (if you have not already completed one) or for the special tax claim form R232.

National Insurance

Children under 16 do not have to pay any National Insurance (NI) contributions. Once 16, Class 1 contributions will be payable for any week in which the child is employed and earns more than the 'weekly lower earnings limit' for the tax year (in 1988–89 the limit is £41 a week). But if a child continues in full-time education after the age of 16, no National Insurance contributions need be paid until he or she is 18. During this period the child will be credited with contributions. The effect of this is that his or her long-term entitlement to benefits will not be affected, but he or she will not become entitled to start receiving most benefits based on NI contributions until at least six months' worth of contributions have actually been paid (more in the case of unemployment benefit – see p.118). Once 18, contributions must be paid in any week in which he or she earns more than the current 'lower earnings limit'. Students of any age on sandwich courses must pay contributions for any weeks they are paid more than the lower earnings limit by their employers.

If a child's source of income counts as self-employment, he or she won't have to pay any National Insurance contributions if he or she is under 16 or is a full-time student under 18. If over 18 or not in full-time education, and his or her earnings from self-employment (after deducting business expenses) in the tax year are expected to be less than a certain amount (in 1988–89 the limit is £2,250), he or she can apply to the DHSS for a certificate of exemption from paying contributions. Otherwise Class 2 National Insurance contributions will have to be paid for each week that he or she does any work for the business. If normally self-employed, he or she will have to pay them for every week. Class 2 contributions are paid at a flat rate which in 1988–89 is £4.05 a week. If he or she makes a profit in the business of more than a certain amount (£4,590 in 1988–89) the child will also have to pay Class 4 National Insurance contributions of 6.3% of the excess up to a maximum contribution of £677.25. However, there is tax relief on half the Class 4 contributions.

Capital gains tax

In the same way as an adult, a child can be liable to capital gains tax if in a tax year he or she sells or gives away things which have increased in value by more than a certain amount since April 1982 or since he acquired them, whichever is later. But it is unlikely in most cases that this will be a practical consideration as your child would have to be very prosperous for this tax to arise, as the first £5,000 of profits made in the tax year are ignored.

Gifts to children

In many cases there will be no repercussions from making gifts of money or property to children, either for the donor or the recipient. But if the value of the gift is very large, there are two considerations:

- If the gift is not of money but is worth more than £3,000 and it has increased in value over the time you have owned it, you could have some capital gains tax to pay if the increase in value since April 1982 or since you acquired it, when added to the other 'gains' you have made in the tax year, come to more than the current threshold for the tax (in 1988–89 this is £5,000). For more details see p.145.
- If the gift is not for your child's education or maintenance, is not a wedding present and is not one of a series of payments out of your income, it could be counted in your estate for inheritance tax purposes if the value of everything you give away in the tax year is over £3,000 and you were to die within seven years. For more details see the details of inheritance tax, as given on the pages beginning p.138.

Gifts from people other than the parents

Before the 1988 Budget, it was possible for people who were not the child's parents to save tax on money they gave a child by making regular payments under a deed of covenant. The effect was that the payer got tax relief on the amount paid over, and the child would not have to pay tax on it if his or her income, including the covenanted payments, came to less than his or her personal tax allowances.

Tax relief will continue to apply to existing covenants which were made before 15 March 1988 and sent to a tax inspector by 30 June 1988. But it is no longer possible to get tax relief on any later new covenants; they are in effect ignored by the tax system, which means that the payer does not get any relief on what he pays, and that for the recipient the money is tax-free.

Children's savings

Most children will want to keep a small part of their money at home in the traditional money box, for spending on small things when they want them. But it makes sense for the rest of the child's money to be put where it can earn some interest. The idea of being paid interest on their savings is often particularly attractive to children, and, more important, it will encourage them to save rather than fritter their money away.

Many children will want to be able to deposit and withdraw fairly small amounts of money, and there are a number of savings schemes which offer this facility. There is, in fact, a lot of competition between institutions for children's savings, largely because they feel that once they have a customer they are likely to keep him or her for a long time – during which the amount that customer has to invest and his or her need for their services will increase substantially. As a result, many banks and building societies have special offers and free gifts for children opening accounts – from money boxes and piggy banks to folders, clipboards, pens, calculators, glossy magazines and competitions. With some accounts older children can get a plastic card for withdrawing money from cash dispensers (up to a maximum of, say, £25 a week), which is probably a good opportunity for some healthy consumer education. Not all these goodies are free and, while you may feel that one or two are worth taking advantage of by depositing the minimum amount of money necessary to qualify, they are not a basis for choosing the best place for the child to invest.

Where to save

For most children the choice of where to put small savings will boil down to a bank, building society, post office or Trustee Savings Bank. The main things for a child to take into account when deciding where to save are:

- Is there a branch near your home or school which you can get to easily, and is it open at convenient times? You could, of course, deal by post but this could prove expensive for a large number of small transactions.
- How much money do you need to open an account, and can you add quite small amounts to your savings if you want to?
- If you want to pay in a regular amount each month, say (perhaps because you earn money from a paper round or are given it under a deed of covenant) do you get a higher-than-normal interest rate? And can you still make withdrawals if you want to? There is often a limit on the number of withdrawals you can make and still get the higher interest rate.
- Can you withdraw money straight away, or do you have to give a certain amount of notice? Do you lose any interest if you do not give the required amount of notice? With most banks' savings accounts you lose seven days' interest if you do not give seven days' notice of withdrawing. With a National Savings Investment Account you need to give a month's notice to withdraw. This may not matter to you if you are using the account for your longer-term savings, and you may even feel it will help you plan your spending and stop you being tempted into withdrawing money for buying things you do not really want on impulse. If you do need money more urgently, you

could probably borrow it from your parents until the withdrawal comes through.
- What rate of interest will be paid on your savings? The higher the rate, the better. You will often find that those offered by banks and building societies are lower than the ones on the National Savings Investment Account, because banks and building societies have to pay tax to the government out of the interest they pay out. Even if your income is too low for you to pay tax, you cannot claim it back. But with National Savings Investment Account no tax is deducted from the interest they pay you, and you only have to pay tax on the interest that is added to your account if your taxable income in the tax year is more than your tax allowances. So for most children National Savings Investment Account will be the better bet as far as interest is concerned.
- Will the interest be paid out to you or added to the amount invested in your account? Interest is usually added to your account, but with some organizations you can ask to have it paid out instead. If it is added, you can of course withdraw it if you want to.
- Will you have to keep your own record of how much you have paid in and withdrawn? With most building society accounts and with National Savings accounts you get a book in which all your deposits and withdrawals are recorded by the counter staff. With banks you normally have to keep your own record, but are sent a statement usually twice a year, listing all the transactions. So in between times you will need to make sure your record is accurate.

Building society share account

You normally need £1 to open a building society share account, after which you can pay money in and draw it out whenever you want to (though you will have to wait for cheques you have paid in to clear – usually 10 to 14 days). If you want to withdraw a very large amount you will normally be given a cheque, but you can ask for this to be made payable to whoever you like, if it is for a payment to someone else. You usually get a passbook in which your transactions are recorded, which makes these accounts very easy for children to use. Societies have different rules about whether you can withdraw at branches other than your usual one. Interest is normally added to your account twice a year, based on the average amount you have had invested. There is no tax to pay on what you get, but you cannot reclaim the tax that the society has paid to the Government. Most building societies offer higher interest rates if you save a regular amount each month or if you invest a lot of money, and they run other types of account which pay more interest but have more restrictions.

Bank children's savings account or deposit account

Bank savings and deposit accounts are much like building society share accounts, except that you normally lose seven days' interest on what you withdraw (unless you give seven days' notice), and you do not normally get a passbook.

National Savings Ordinary Account

You can open a National Savings Ordinary Account at any Savings Bank post office with £1. You get a passbook in which the counter staff enter your transactions. You can withdraw up to £100 in cash on demand at any of these post offices, but when you withdraw more than £50 your book is kept for checking. You can withdraw larger amounts by post. Interest is only paid on each whole pound for each calendar month it is invested, and the interest rate is very low – normally only 2.5%. But if you have the account for a whole calendar year, the interest rate becomes 5% in calendar months in which you have £500 or more in the account. Interest is added at the end of each year, and up to £70 of interest is tax-free in each tax year. But for most people, the low interest rate will mean that National Savings Ordinary Account is not worth considering.

National Savings Investment Account

The Investment Account is a rather different kettle of fish from the National Savings Ordinary Account. You need £5 to open one, which you can do at any Savings Bank post office, and you also get a passbook in which your transactions are recorded. You can pay in money at post offices at any time, but you have to give a month's notice to withdraw. To do this you get a form from a post office and send it off (post free). You are then sent either a cheque or a warrant which you can cash at a post office a month later. Interest is earned on each whole pound for each day it is invested, and is added to the account at the end of each year. The interest rate on National Savings Investment Account is generally quite a bit higher than banks or building societies offer, so it is well worth considering for your child's longer-term savings. The interest is taxable, but this will not affect most children: tax would only be payable if the interest they received in the tax year, when added to their other taxable income, came to more than their personal tax allowance (£2,605 in 1988–89).

Conclusions on where to save

National Savings Investment Account will normally pay your child the most interest, and is best for money he or she is not going to want for a few months or will not want to withdraw in frequent small amounts.

A building society account (or bank account if more convenient) is very useful for money he or she wants to pay in and take out more frequently.

There is no reason why your child should not have both these – and probably keep a small amount of cash at home as well.

Investing for children

If you have a lot of money to invest for your child (or someone else's) to give him or her a nest egg when reaching adulthood, or if you are an older child with money to invest on a longer-term basis, there are better options than those listed above.

With each type of investment there is a minimum age at which a child can invest in his own right. You can open National Savings accounts in a child's name at any age, but withdrawals are not normally allowed until the child is seven. The same may apply with accounts at banks or, like building societies, you may find that you cannot open an account in the name of a child under a certain age, normally also seven. Children cannot usually hold shares or unit trusts in their own name until they are 18, nor can they buy British Government stock through a stockbroker (though they can buy them through a post office). Life insurance companies have varying rules about the age at which children can take out policies.

You can, however, buy investments or open an account *on behalf of* a child of any age, in which case both your name and the child's often appear on the documents. The income from these investments can only be used for the benefit of the child, and if you are the parent and the income in a tax year is more than £5 it will be treated for tax purposes as if it was your income.

An investment you have made on behalf of a child normally becomes the child's property when he or she is 18. But if you want to you can hand it over earlier as long as the child has reached the minimum age for that investment.

If you transfer investments of yours (such as shares or unit trusts) to a child, there could be capital gains tax to pay if those investments have increased in value in the period you have owned them. Any gain which accrues after you have handed them over will be regarded as the child's. See p.145 for more details.

When you invest money on your child's behalf or hand over investments to them, this counts as a gift to the child for inheritance tax purposes, meaning that the value of the gift would be included in your taxable estate if you were to die within seven years, unless the value fell within one of the exemptions from inheritance tax. See p.142 for more details.

Choosing an investment

The choice of investment is likely to depend to some extent on whether the investment (or the money for it) is being given by the parents or coming from another source (such as a grandparent, or the child's own earnings). If the money is coming from the parents, the income from the investments will be counted as theirs, so the investments can be chosen on much the same basis as the parents would choose investments for themselves over a similar period. So if the parents pay income tax, and particularly if they pay it at the higher rate, it will be worth going for investments where what you get back is tax-free (e.g. National Savings Certificates and Yearly Plan, and most life insurance policies) or where most or all of the return is capital gain rather than income, for example certain unit trusts and low-coupon British Government stock (which is always free of capital gains tax). Alternatively, you might consider buying quality heirlooms like antique silver or furniture to hand down to your children.

If, however, the investments are being provided from a source other than the parents, the income from them will be regarded as the child's for tax purposes, so the choice of investment will depend to some extent on the child's tax position. If, as will normally be the case, the child's income is not high enough to pay any income tax and income-producing investments are required, it will be worth going for ones where either no tax is deducted from what is paid out (for example, National Savings accounts and bonds) or where any tax deducted can be reclaimed (such as shares, unit trusts, British Government stock). Investments where tax is deducted and cannot be reclaimed (as with banks and building societies) will be less attractive, but investments where most of what you get back is capital gain will still be worth considering.

The next consideration is that if you are investing for a child you will normally be investing for the long-term – i.e. 10 or 15 years or more. Picking the combination of investments which will give the best return over such a long period of time is of course a combination of good judgement and good luck. And a high return is not the only thing you are looking for: those investments which have shown high returns in the past are, of course, often the riskiest – they are the very same ones as might also have shown the lowest returns or become worthless. Whereas money in a building society will grow gradually, the value of the shares in a particular company may multiply tenfold, stagnate or even become worthless. Over the period from 1974 to 1987 the average investment in shares or unit trusts would have brought a much higher return than investing in a bank or building society or in fixed interest stocks. But in the early seventies the position was quite different, as most shares and stocks just want down and down in value, and the fall on 'Black Monday' in October 1987 was a sharp reminder that share prices can fall as well as rise.

Another risk which affects the return on investments is inflation. If the rate of inflation is higher than the return being paid on an investment (as was true for much of the seventies) the value of your investment is effectively going down – because you won't be able to buy as much with the money at the end as you could at the outset. This does not mean that it is not worth investing, as any return on your money is better than none at all; but it does mean that when you are investing for the longer-term, in which it is impossible to feel confident about the rate of inflation for more than a year or two ahead, some of your money should be put into index-linked investments. There are two main investments of this type. With Index-Linked National Savings Certificates the value of each certificate is increased in line with the Retail Price Index (RPI – the Government's measure of inflation) and interest is added on top of that. With Index-Linked British Government stock, both the capital invested and the amounts of the interest paid out are guaranteed to keep pace with inflation. Although the mechanics of how these stocks work are complicated, they are easy enough to invest in and are the best protection you can get against the ravages of long-term inflation.

In the light of all this, it will therefore normally be good policy to get a fair chunk of money in relatively safe investments before branching out into more risky ones. So the first things to consider would be:

- a with-profits life insurance policy written in trust for the child (see p.141)
- British Government stock (including index-linked ones) with a redemption date around the time the child will come of age (choose low-coupon stock if the money comes from the child's parents and the father pays tax)
- bank and building society savings accounts (if the money comes from the child's parents and they are taxpayers)
- National Savings Certificates (including index-linked ones) and National Savings Deposit Bonds (if the money does not come from the child's parents).

When you are wanting to invest more, you could consider investments which have a greater chance of earning a higher return, as long as you also appreciate that there are greater risks involved. These might include:

- a unit-linked life insurance policy written in trust for the child
- British Government stock (including index-linked ones) with various redemption dates
- unit trusts
- shares in investment trust companies
- ordinary shares in companies
- 'alternative' investments, such as antiques, port, coins, precious metals.

With investments of this type it is too much to expect to do well on all of them, and what you should aim at is to do better overall than you would have done on less risky investments. This will mean reducing the risk of doing very badly by spreading money between several investments – the riskier they are, the more there should be. A unit trust or investment trust does this for you to some extent, as each trust will invest in a large number of different stocks and shares. But you can reduce the risk still further by investing in more than one unit trust and more than one type of riskier investment.

Life insurance policies
When you take out a life insurance policy, you have the option of having it 'written in trust' for someone you name. Then if you were to die during the term of the policy, the proceeds of the policy would be paid straight to that person. If the policy involved investment (for example, an endowment policy) the investment proceeds would be payable to the named person when the policy matured. However, in either of these cases, if the named person was a child who was then under 18, the proceeds would be held in trust for the child until he or she reached 18. Ask the life insurance company about having the policy written in trust; it does not cost anything and you may be able to get an existing policy changed if you want to.

An investment-type insurance policy on a parent's life written in trust for a child is therefore both useful protection in the event of the parent dying and a way of providing a nest-egg for a child. It also has other advantages. The premiums will normally fall well within the annual amounts exempt from inheritance tax (see p.142), so that they would not be added to your taxable estate if you were to die within seven years. And once money is paid into the policy, any growth in value belongs to the trust, so you will not be taxed on it (see below). When the child receives the benefits, they will normally be free of any tax.

Accumulation and maintenance trusts
It can be worth setting up a trust if you want to hand over a substantial amount of money or property to other people but do not want them to have full control over the assets for some

time. Trusts are useful for passing property on to children, grandchildren, nephews, nieces and so on because you can save them substantial amounts of inheritance tax by giving away things in your lifetime without your losing control over what happens to them.

A trust is a type of fund which can own money, investments or other things in its own right, independently of any individual. The person who starts it is called the settlor. The settlor gives things or money to the trust and gets a trust deed drawn up by a solicitor giving the rules for running the trust and saying who is to benefit from it (the beneficiaries). The settlor will also need to appoint trustees who are responsible for running the trust in accordance with the rules and with the law. To keep control of the property in the trust, the settlor can himself be a trustee. If a solicitor is appointed, he or she can charge for the service provided. The money and property in the trust belong to the trust for the time being (not to the trustees, they merely look after it), but it will eventually be transferred to the beneficiaries.

An accumulation and maintenance trust is a special type of trust for benefitting children. You normally start the trust when they are young (you cannot start it before any are born). Over time, the value of property in the trust will hopefully increase and the trust will earn interest on its investments. Any income earned by the investments in the trust can either be kept in the trust and reinvested or can be paid out to provide for the maintenance or education of the beneficiaries (i.e. your chidren) but it cannot be used for any other purpose.

An accumulation and maintenance trust is not only for the settlor's children; it can be established for any children, but it cannot last for more than 25 years unless all the beneficiaries have a grandparent in common. But in any case at least one of the beneficiaries must become entitled to start receiving the income from the trust before their 25th birthday. The capital can be kept in the trust for longer, but all the trust's income and capital must eventually be handed over to them.

The main advantage in setting up an accumulation and maintenance trust for your children is that it can mean much less inheritance tax to pay. Although the gifts you make into the trust would be liable to inheritance tax if you were to die within seven years of making them, the chance of your dying then is much less than it is when your children are in their twenties; also, the tax would be worked out on the value of the gift at the time you put it into the trust, not its value at the time of death. There is no inheritance tax when the things in the trust are passed on to your children.

Trustees have to pay tax at 35% on any investment income which the trust receives. If the income is accumulated in the trust that is the end of the story, though bear in mind that if you pay tax only at the basic rate of 25%, the rate at which the investments grow will be slower in a trust than out. However, income which the trustees pay out to the beneficiaries is normally treated as theirs – so if they were not liable to pay any tax they could reclaim all the tax that the trustees had deducted. The exception is that if you set up the trust for your own children, income paid out for their education or maintenance while they are under 18 and unmarried is taxed as though it was your income. However, if you have set up one of these trusts for your children and they are under 18, for tax years in which you pay only basic rate tax it is best to ask the trustees to pay out as much of the trust's income as possible that year for the education and maintenance of the children. You can then reclaim the difference between the 35% tax paid by the trustees and the 25% tax you would be liable for.

Trustees also have to pay capital gains tax on any capital gains made by the trust at 35%, and the threshold at which a trust starts to pay this tax is half of that for an individual.

Trusts are complicated and expensive to set up, they cost money to run and you would certainly need advice from a solicitor. He should also be able to advise you on whether a trust is worthwhile in your circumstances.

8 Safeguarding the family's future

The two main risks which any family face are the parents losing the ability to look after the children and the ability to support the family financially. Either may be caused by death, accident, disablement or long-term illness, and the second may be caused by unemployment. The State sometimes helps out in these situations and there are various types of insurance available to fill the gaps, some of which are very valuable and not expensive.

Death of a parent

Although death is statistically unlikely for most people at the ages at which they have dependent children, its effects would be far-reaching and must be considered and insured against. Fortunately, because it is an unlikely event for most people, it is cheap to buy a substantial amount of insurance.

Because it is more common for the man to be the main breadwinner in a family, it is usually the case that men have much more life insurance cover than women. Not only is cover more likely to be provided by the man's employer as one of the benefits of his firm's pension scheme, but much insurance company literature is aimed at men taking out policies to benefit their wives and children. It is very important for a father to have this cover, but it is seldom realized that it can also be important for a mother. There are several reasons for this:

- If a man dies, as long as his National Insurance contribution record was sufficient, his wife will become entitled to widow's benefits including, if she has dependent children, widowed mother's allowance. Depending on her age, these benefits can provide her with a guaranteed income from the time of her husband's death to the time she retires. The only direct benefit a man with dependent children will get from the State when his wife dies is one-parent benefit (worth only £4.90 a week in 1988–89).
- If, as is usual, the father has worked for more years and on higher pay than the mother, any lump sum and pension paid to his widow on his death are likely to be much higher than any lump sum and widower's pension he would receive from his wife's employer's pension scheme.
- Even if the wife has little or no income, her role in running the home and looking after the children would be a very expensive one for the husband to replace if she were to die. Without any insurance cover on her life, a father might have to give up his job and live on social security in order to be able to look after his children.

Single parents and unmarried couples need life insurance even more – in the latter case because the woman will not get any State widow's benefits, though she may get dependent's benefits from an employer's pension scheme.

Types of life insurance

The most important type of life insurance – and by far the cheapest – is called 'term insurance', because it only pays out if you die within a fixed term (if you survive the period you get nothing back). By far the most important period is while you have dependent children, so you will want a policy which lasts until all your children are likely to be off your hands.

There are two types of term insurance. One pays out a tax-free lump sum, so if you take out a £25,000 20-year policy it will pay out a single lump sum of £25,000 if you die within the 20-year period. The other type of policy is called a 'family income benefit' policy, and pays out a tax-free income from the time you die until the end of the period of the policy. So if you were to die in the fifth year of a 20-year policy, it would pay out an income for the next 15 years. The income can either be level or can increase each year, usually at a fixed rate (such as 5% or 10% a year, or in line with inflation), to provide some compensation for inflation. As your partner may depend on the income for a good many years, this is an important factor. A lump sum policy has a built-in compensation for inflation: if you were to die in the later years, prices would be higher than if you died earlier, but the same amount of money would need to last for fewer years.

It does not matter too much whether you go for a lump sum policy or a family income benefit policy. A lump sum can be invested to provide an income, and with an income policy the insurance company may well be prepared to pay out a lump sum instead. You will find the cost of, say, 20-year policies which provide either a lump sum of £20,000, or an income of £1,000 in the first year and increasing each year, are not very different. Either policy from a cheap company would cost a 30-year-old man or a 34-year-old woman about £3 a month.

The cover you need
Before taking out a life insurance policy, you should work out roughly how much capital and how much income your partner and children would need if you were to die. First add up how much capital your partner would need to have available. This should include funeral expenses (£500 or more), loans he or she would want to be repaid (e.g. any mortgage or bank loan, if these are not already covered by life insurance), and some spare cash. Then add up how much capital would be available on your death – from life insurance you already have, from your

employer's pension scheme, from savings and investments your partner will inherit and from selling anything of yours they would not want to keep (such as your car). If the total that would be available is less than the total capital your partner would need, the cover on your life should provide a lump sum at least equal to the shortfall. If it is more, the excess can be used to provide some of the income your partner would need after your death, or it can simply be considered as a useful bonus.

The next step is to consider the income your partner and children would need. First, add up the income you get – your take-home pay, any state benefits you get, any income from investments which your partner would cash in or sell, and any other income which would cease on your death. If your partner would need to employ someone in the home to replace what you do, add on what it would cost to employ them. And if they would need to give up work or work for fewer hours, add on the income they would lose. From this total subtract the amount of State benefits your partner would get and any income he or she would get from your employer's pension scheme. Also subtract the repayments on any loan which would be paid off on your death (like mortgage payments) and any other costs which would be saved, like transport to work. The amount you have left is the additional income your partner would need.

It is up to you and your partner how you decide to match the risks to the policies. You may think it is worth rounding up the amounts you will need quite considerably if you can afford the premiums; you may decide that a combination of lump sum and income would suit you best. If you are unsure, a lump sum is more flexible, as some or all of it can be invested to provide a regular income or to be drawn on as required.

Arranging your insurance

The cost of insurance varies widely between insurance companies – the most expensive often costs more than double the cheapest – but the product you get is virtually identical. So it is always worth looking in the most recent report on life insurance in *Which?* magazine (available at libraries) to find the cheapest companies. When you apply for the insurance you normally have to give detailed information about your health, and if this has not been good you may find companies want to charge you extra or will not even insure you at all. So quite a bit of shopping around may be necessary.

Many companies offer more expensive policies which allow you to take out more insurance in the future even if your health has deteriorated in the meantime. The main options are to be able to renew the policy at the end, to increase the amount of cover you get, and to convert to another type of policy (i.e., one which involves investment) with the same company.

Don't be talked into options you do not need – most life insurance representatives and brokers get commission on the policies they sell, and the more you pay the more they get. Similarly, don't be talked into buying policies which last longer than you need, nor into buying investment-type policies which are very much more expensive if your main need is for protection.

If both you and your partner need insurance, you may be offered a joint-life policy. There are two types – those which pay out on the first death, and those which pay out on the second. If you go for one of these, you would need the first type, unless you want to leave the money to your children, who may well be grown up by then. However, because policies are generally taken out for between 10 and 25 years and it is anyone's guess what will happen in such a long period, it is generally better for you each to take out a separate policy on your own life written in trust for your partner. The cost of the two policies is not likely to be much more than one joint-life policy, and in some cases may even be slightly less.

If either of you is self-employed or is in a job in which you do not belong to an employer's pension scheme, you can get tax relief on life assurance premiums of up to 5% of the amount you are being taxed on in that tax year which comes from this self-employment or non-pensionable job. Tell the life insurance company you want a *Section 226A* policy, and they will give you a certificate to send to your tax office to claim your tax relief.

It will nearly always be worthwhile to have policies 'written in trust' for your partner or children. The insurance money can then be paid promptly after the death, and free of any inheritance tax. See p.141 for more details.

Policies which include investment

Instead of buying term insurance, which only pays out if you die, you can pay more and have most of what you pay invested by the insurance company so that when the policy comes to an end you are paid out of the proceeds of the invested funds. The three main types of these policies are endowment policies (either with-profit or non-profit), unit-linked policies, and whole life policies.

Life insurance companies and their agents are very keen to sell policies of these types, and will provide you with plenty of glossy literature about them. But there are several drawbacks in considering these for protecting your family:
- they may cost up to 20 times as much (or even more) for the same amount of insurance protection
- you are committing yourself to pay a substantial amount of money for a long period of time
- in that time, more profitable investment opportunities might present themselves
- even if you can afford the premiums now, if you fell on hard times you would get very poor value if you had to cash in your policy early.

Endowment and unit-linked policies may be useful ways of *investing* for children (see p.101) and whole-life policies may possibly be useful for paying a large inheritance tax bill (see p.141), but they are not the best ways of *protecting* a family.

For this purpose you would do best to keep your life insurance and your investments quite separate.

Illness, injury and accident

While life insurance attracts a lot of interest and many people arrange one kind or another, far fewer people consider how they and their family would manage if they were to suffer a long-term illness or become permanently disabled. Yet the chance of this happening is far greater than the chance of death, and the financial implications can be just as bad, so protection is very important for anyone with dependents. Some lucky people may, however, find that their employer gives them very good protection as a tax-free perk of the job. What you get from the State depends on whether you are in a job, self-employed or unemployed. Information is given in the DHSS leaflet FB.28 *Sick or Disabled*.

If you are in a job

If you are unable to work through illness, your employer will in most cases pay you statutory sick pay for up to 28 weeks. This is a taxable payment from the State which in 1988–89 is a weekly amount of £34.25 if you ean £41 to £79.49 a week, or £49.20 if you earn £79.50 or more a week. You do not qualify for statutory sick pay at all if you earn less than £41 a week, you are not working because of a trade dispute, or you are waiting to start a new job; there are also some other exceptions. Tell your employer you are ill straight away – your employer should organize your statutory sick pay or explain what you must do if you don't qualify.

If you do not get statutory sick pay, you may qualify for sickness benefit for the first 28 weeks of your illness. You qualify for this if you have paid or have been credited with enough National Insurance contributions in the previous two tax years or if your inability to work was caused by an industrial accident or disease. The amount in 1988–89 is only £31.30

plus another £19.40 for an adult dependent, but these payments are tax-free. If you're over pension age you get more – in 1988–89 the amount is £39.45 plus £23.65 for an adult dependent and £8.40 for any dependent child. Claim on form SC.1 from your employer, the DHSS, your doctor's surgery or hospital.

If you are still unable to work after 28 weeks you can get invalidity benefit for as long as you are off work – there is no time limit on this. The basic amount in 1988–89 is £41.15 a week, but you may be entitled to receive more in certain circumstances.

If your illness or disablement was caused by an accident at work or by a recognized industrial disease, you may get compensation from your employer's insurer. You may also get higher levels of benefits than those above. More information is given in DHSS leaflet FB.15 *Injured at Work* which explains the various benefits available and tells you which other leaflets describe each benefit in detail.

In addition to these benefits from the State, your employers may provide a sick pay insurance scheme, or if you are unable to work again the firm's pension scheme may allow you to retire early and get a pension on favourable terms. A good sick pay scheme will make your statutory sick pay up to your full salary for the first six months you are off work, and after that will make any State benefits you get up to half or two-thirds your normal pay indefinitely – up to retirement age if necessary. It will also increase the amount you get each year to compensate for inflation, and will pay your contributions to the firm's pension scheme for as long as you are off work. So you will need to check up on whether your employer has such a scheme, whether you qualify for the benefits (you may need to have worked for the firm for a certain time), how much you would be paid if you were off work, how long the payments would last on both full rate and on a reduced rate, and whether they would increase each year. The money paid out by such a scheme is normally taxable.

If you belong to a trade union, you may find that it will provide some benefits if you are unable to work through illness.

If you are self-employed
If you have paid enough Class 2 National Insurance contributions in the previous tax year, you will qualify for sickness benefit for the first 28 weeks you are unable to work, followed by invalidity benefit after that. The weekly amounts are as above.

If you are not in work
You may be able to claim sickness benefit and invalidity benefit if you were in a job or self-employed in the previous tax year and paid enough National Insurance contributions to qualify. If you did not, you may still be able to get severe disablement allowance when you have been unable to work for 28 weeks. But unless you're registered blind or partially sighted or are receiving a benefit such as attendance allowance, if you were 20 or over when you first became unable to work you must be regarded as at least 80% disabled to qualify. The allowance is a tax-free payment of £24.75 a week plus £13.90 for an adult dependent and £8.40 for each dependent child. If you need a lot of looking after you may be able to get attendance allowance as well (generally £22 a week in 1988–89 but may be higher if you need 24-hour care – £32.95 a week). If you are unable or virtually unable to walk you may also get mobility allowance (£23.05 a week in 1988–89).

Permanent Health Insurance
Unless you work for an employer with a generous sick pay scheme, it is likely that you will need some insurance to cover the possibility of long-term illness or permanent disability. This is particularly the case if you are self-employed, when you might have to confront how to support your family while unable to work. The type of insurance which best fills the gap

is permanent health insurance (PHI), which will pay you an income for as long as you are too ill to work. It is called permanent for two reasons: first, because once you have taken out a policy the company cannot refuse to renew your insurance if your health becomes worse or if you claim on the policy; second, because if you are permanently disabled the policy will continue to pay out until you reach State pension age (though you can save money by agreeing an earlier age if you want to – as with life insurance you may consider that the most important period is while you have dependent children). The policy may pay a reduced income if you are able to work part-time or only able to do a lower-paid job.

You can choose how much cover you want, but generally the insurance company will try to see that your total income (including any State benefits you get) while you are off work is not more than about three-quarters of your normal pay (so that you are not tempted to stay off work longer than is necessary). So there is no point in over-insuring.

You also choose a 'waiting period' – the time when you are first ill but before the policy starts paying out. For example, if your employer's scheme covers you adequately for the first six months you are ill but offers little after that, you would choose a waiting period of six months. The longer the waiting period, the cheaper the insurance.

With some policies, the income the policy will pay out stays the same forever, which is not much use if you first claim in ten years time after a period of high inflation. So unless you are near to retirement age, it is better to pay more for a policy where the income the company will pay out increases each year, both before and after a claim. The income paid out by a permanent health policy is tax-free until the second 5th April after it starts being paid, after which it is taxable.

When deciding how much income you want the policy to pay out, you will need to consider how much you will get from your employer and the State, whether your partner works (and could continue working with you off ill), how much you will need for the children, and so on. The cost of the insurance depends on your age, sex, occupation, health record, the waiting period, the number of years you insure for, and whether the income paid out increases as time goes on. For example, a policy which pays out £100 a week initially, increased in line with inflation until retirement age, might cost a 30-year-old man around £90 a year, a woman about £10 more. A 45-year-old might have to pay nearly twice as much.

Not many companies will insure people who do not have any earnings, such as housewives and the unemployed. But two companies that will offer housewives policies where the income increases are Permanent (tel: 01-636 1686) and Phoenix (tel: 0272 277788).

Accident insurance

A cheaper alternative to PHI is to take out accident insurance only. This is cheaper because statistically the injuries covered are very unlikely. These policies pay out a lump sum if you are involved in an accident and are killed or permanently disabled or lose an eye or a limb. Or if you are off work as the result of an accident, they will pay you an income for up to two years. Some policies will pay both a lump sum and an income, and some have wider cover still. Some pay out an income if you are in hospital or if you are off work through illness.

However, these policies are not adequate in themselves. As an income is only paid for two years they do not offer the long-term protection of PHI. Another snag is that if you claim on the policy you may find yourself unable to renew it.

Accident insurance is, however, well worth taking out for your children. If one of your children was injured in an accident you could be faced with medical costs, lost earnings while you look after the child, the cost of nursing care, and so on. This insurance can cost very little – for example, a policy for school children issued through Brown Shipley Schools (0444 458144) costs £10 a year for up to £50,000 of cover, or £18 a year for up to £100,000 cover for each child.

Out of work

If you are made redundant from a job you have been in for at least two years since the age of 18, your employer must normally pay you a redundancy payment. The amount you are legally entitled to is not large and depends upon your age, the number of years you have worked for the firm and your pay (up to a maximum of £164 per week in 1988–89). The most you can get as a legal requirement in 1988–89 is £4,920 (if you are aged 61 or over and have worked for the firm for 20 years) but many employers have redundancy schemes which offer considerably more than the minimum legal requirement, and there is no reason why you should not ask for more. Payments you get when you are made redundant or dismissed can normally be arranged so that they are tax-free up to £30,000.

If you do not have a job but want to get one you may be able to claim unemployment benefit. It is not enough to have just lost your job – you must in the past have paid or been credited with enough National Insurance contributions of the right type. From October 1988 the conditions will be tougher – you will have to have actually paid (credits will not do) National Insurance contributions while in a job for at least six months out of the two tax years ending in the April before you claim. Until then, it is possible to get benefit following a period of study or illness or disablement, provided that you have actually paid NI contributions while working for at least six months during any tax year since April 1975.

You claim unemployment benefit at an unemployment benefit office. You should do so on your first day of unemployment as claims cannot usually be backdated. However, you do not get any benefit for the first three days of unemployment – the first 26 weeks if you did not have to leave your last job or if you were dismissed for misconduct. You will normally have to return to 'sign on' every week or fortnight, unless you're aged 60 or over or have dependent children under 16. If you are over 18 you do not have to register at a Jobcentre, though it is clearly sensible to do so. Unemployment benefit is only paid for one year, after which your only recourse will be to other State benefits (see chapter 3).

In 1988–89 the standard rate of benefit is £32.75 a week if you're under pension age, £41.15 if you're over. There is an extra £20.20 a week for an adult dependent (£24.75 if you're over pension age), but with unemployment benefit there is no extra for dependent children, unless you are over the State pension age when you can get £8.40 a week for each child. For help with covering their costs you have to apply for other benefits, such as income support (see p.44).

There is little generally available insurance against unemployment. Presumably insurance companies consider the risk too high or too hard to quantify. You can, however, sometimes find insurance schemes which cover specific payments (like the repayments on a loan) if you become unemployed. This may be worth having if you think the chances of losing your job are quite high, but probably not otherwise. (But you can't take out unemployment insurance if you know you are likely to lose your job.)

The message is that to provide the best protection for you and your family against unemployment, it is worth trying while you are in a job to persuade your employer to make his redundancy terms as favourable as possible. You can do this through your trade union or staff association. If you are losing your job, try to get the best possible compensation for yourself that you can – you have nothing to lose. And try to make sure that it is paid to you in such a way that it is tax-free rather than taxable. The personnel manager or company accountant should know how to arrange this.

9 Education and after

State education may in itself be free, but there are a good many costs associated with it. They are not all essential but one is likely to feel that one's own children are missing out compared with others if they are not pretty well all met. As well as the cost of uniforms or school clothes, there may be some transport costs, the cost of providing them with all the equipment they need (writing, drawing, sports, musical or whatever), books you think they need, educational visits, school outings and trips abroad; not to mention all the contributions you end up making to school facilities through fund-raising events and activities. This is not to say that one should object to making any such contribution to one's child's activities, but when the money goes in dribs and drabs it is easy to overlook how much it may add up to.

However, with State education the major cost is met by the Government out of taxes. Parents who opt for private education are saddling themselves with much higher bills. Of course, there is the basic cost of the fees, but all these 'extras' not only have to be met, but are often more expensive than in the State system. There are ways of lessening the burden of fees, as there is help you may be able to get towards some of the costs of State education.

Help from the local authority

There are several ways in which local education authorities (LEAs) may help out with the ancillary costs of education. LEAs are the sections of local councils (normally the county council or metropolitan district council) which organize education. In inner London, the Inner London Education Authority (ILEA) runs education until April 1990, when the London boroughs take over responsibility. Each area has its own rules about the benefits, so you will have to ask locally about which benefits are available in your area and under what circumstances you qualify.

Fares to school

In most areas the LEA provides school buses or issues free passes to cover public transport fares for children under eight who live more than two miles from their nearest school and children aged eight or over who live more than three miles away.

Free school meals and milk

LEAs no longer have to provide either meals or milk at school, except that they must provide free mid-day meals for children whose parents are getting income support. For other children it is up to the authority whether they lay on any milk and meals at all and, if they do, how much they charge and how much they subsidise them out of the rates (if at all). They are allowed to charge less for certain children but they do not have to.

Grants for school clothing

Many LEAs will provide school uniforms, shoes and sports clothes for children from low-income families, or will give grants towards their cost. The amount they will pay depends on your income, and you may have to pay part of the cost.

Educational maintenance allowances

Many local education authorities will pay a small grant to low-income families who have a child under 19 still studying to 'A'-level or Ordinary National Diploma standard (or below) full-time after school-leaving age. It is paid on top of child benefit, and will be disregarded for getting income support or family credit. The authority will want to be satisfied that the child is following a suitable course, and the amount of grant they pay will depend on your income and circumstances. There is no guarantee of getting one – they are entirely at the authority's discretion.

Help from your employer

Some employers pay scholarships to their employees to cover or go towards the costs of educating their children. For example, if your employer requires you to work away from home for a long period, he may pay the costs of your children going to a boarding school for that time. The scholarship will not be regarded as your child's income, so he or she will not have to pay any tax on it. Instead it will be treated by the taxman as a fringe benefit you get with your job, so will you have to pay tax on the amount of the scholarship?

The answer is no if you do not earn more than £708 a month or £163 a week. 'Earnings' here means what you are paid including overtime pay, tips, bonuses, commission etc, plus any expenses which your employer repays to you and the taxable value of any fringe benefits you get.

If you earn more than this, the scholarship will only be tax-free if it was awarded before 15 March 1983, the first payment was made before 6 April 1984 and the child is still studying full-time at the same school or college. Otherwise you will be taxed on the amount your employer pays. Of course, even though the total amount of tax payable could be quite high, this is still preferable to having to pay the whole cost of the child's private education yourself.

Planning for school fees

If you intend to send a child to an independent school, it is worth considering many years in advance how you are going to pay for it. If you have a high income and have just one child whom you want to attend on a daily basis, you may well be able to afford the fees out of your income. But if you are going to have more than one child boarding at independent schools at the same time you will probably need to start planning many years in advance if you are not pretty wealthy.

In 1987–88, the yearly fees charged by many independent schools fell in these ranges:

	Junior	Senior
Day	£1,000 – £1,500	£1,500 – £3,000
Boarder	£2,000 – £3,000	£3,500 – £5,000

So the total fees for a child to board at an independent school for the seven years of secondary education could come to over £30,000. That is in today's money, of course; like most other things school fees are likely to go up each year, so it would not be any good simply to save up £30,000. But with some guidelines you can work out how much you need to invest now to provide for the future.

Suppose your child is at present just a baby and you assume that in the next 18 years school fees are going to go up in line with the rate of inflation and that over that period you can get a return on your investments of 3% above the rate of inflation (as you currently can with Index-linked National Savings Certificates and Index-Linked British Government stock). You would need to invest a lump sum of around £21,000 now to provide the funds for your baby to spend the seven years of secondary education at an independent school currently charging £4,500 a year. You can change these figures pro rata, so if the school you have in mind currently charges £3,000 a year you would need to invest £14,000.

Instead of investing a large lump sum you could make a smaller investment each year. For example, if you wanted your baby to go to a £4,500-a-year secondary school and you wanted to spread the cost over the first twelve years of his or her life, you would need to invest around £2,000 in the first year, and in each of the 11 subsequent years invest the same amount again but increased by the current rate of inflation. This assumes you then leave the money invested and earning interest until you need to withdraw some each year to pay the fees.

If you wanted to spread the cost over the 18 years from birth until the child left the school you would only need to invest £1,500 in the first year. Again, you would need to increase the amount you invested each year by the current rate of inflation. From the eleventh year onwards, instead of investing the current equivalent of £1,500, you would pay it to the school to cover part of the fees and would pay the rest by withdrawing from the invested money. Again, you can change these figures pro rata, so if the school currently charges £3,000 a year the first year's investment need be only £1,000.

Of course, these guidelines will only hold true if the assumptions they are based on turn out to be correct. If school fees raced ahead of average inflation, or if the real return on investments fell, you would have to invest more. And if you could not afford to invest as much as was necessary each year your child might have to wait a year or two longer before going to the school.

Some independent schools have schemes whereby you can make payments in advance, perhaps to a charitable trust. The money is invested, usually in an annuity, which pays part or all of the fees each year your child is at the school.

School fees schemes
Various insurance companies and insurance brokers offer off-the-peg schemes specifically designed for saving up for school fees in ways similar to those described above. They do not guarantee that enough money will be available to pay the fees

of any particular school, but they do make sure that money will be available at the times when the fees become due.

There are a number of different types of plan available, some much more flexible than others, so it is sensible to find out about several and choose the one most suited to your circumstances. For example, there are schemes where your payments start low but increase each year, others where they stay constant, and others which allow you to make a lump sum payment initially and add to it at intervals later. With some schemes the amount of money paid out is guaranteed from the start, while with others it will depend on the success of the investments.

Many schemes involve either an annuity or a series of insurance policies. An annuity is an investment which pays out a fixed income for a set period, in this case beginning when the child starts at the school and finishing when he or she leaves. Schemes which involve insurance usually have a series of policies ending in consecutive years. If you invest a lump sum, the money may be put into a selection of other investments and then some withdrawn to pay the policy premiums each year. If there are only a few years to go before the child is due to start at the school, the investments may be used to pay the fees directly.

There are other differences too. With some schemes a trust is set up to hold the money invested, and payments may be made direct to the school. You may be asked if you want to retain the right to cash in the investments, or if you are prepared to give this up; this could affect the inheritance tax position if you were to die. Some schemes are more effective than others if you pay tax at the higher rate. With all these variations, it is very important to get thorough advice from the people arranging the plan.

Even if you are intending to arrange your own investments it is worth finding out about these schemes as they may give you ideas for suitable types of investment to use and in what ways. Some of these companies advertise in *The Independent Schools*

Yearbook which your library will probably have. They are also listed in a leaflet called *School Fees* produced by The Independent Schools Information Service (ISIS) (tel: 01-630 8793).

If you decide to send your child to an independent school when it is too late to invest in this way, you may be able to borrow some or all of the money for the fees and pay it back over the next 10 to 25 years. You can get details of such a scheme from ISIS.

Leaving school

The majority of children leaving school will be looking for jobs. Some will go on to full-time education (see next section), but those who do not get jobs and do not become students need not be left wholly unemployed. They can take up a place on the Youth Training Scheme or take part-time further education courses. Alternatively they can consider a job on the community programme, doing voluntary work or even starting their own small business. But many may be unemployed for the initial period after leaving school.

Unemployed

It is important that anyone without a job registers as unemployed as soon as possible. People over 18 should sign on at the local unemployment benefit office. Those under 18 have to register for work at their local careers office or Jobcentre, who will arrange an appointment at the unemployment benefit office. However, school-leavers cannot get unemployment benefit, because entitlement depends partly on having paid enough National Insurance contributions in a previous tax year. Until 1 September 1988 they will be able to claim income support from the beginning of the term after they leave school. After this, school-leavers will not be entitled to benefit while aged under 18 – they will continue to be offered places under the Youth Training Scheme or other scheme until they take one up or reach the age of 18. Income support can be paid straight away to someone who is aleady 19, who is disabled, who has a child, or who lives away from home and is not supported by their parents. Doing casual work will mean losing unemployment benefit for any day (except Sundays) on which more than £2 is earned, and income support is lost if the claimant earns more than £5 a week. It is therefore better to earn as much as possible on certain days (or weeks) and do no work on other days – but your child needs to be careful, because if he or she regularly works the same hours each week, this will be treated as normal working pattern and he or she won't get benefit. However, doing voluntary work will not normally affect how much benefit is paid. For more about income support see p.44; for unemployment benefit see p.118.

Youth Training Scheme

Anyone who leaves school at 16 has a right to two years' training on the Youth Training Scheme (YTS). Those who leave at 17 have a right to at least a year on the scheme, as does any disabled person under 21. There are various schemes in each area, run by the Manpower Services Commission, colleges, employers, local councils, etc. Information about them can be obtained from local careers offices or Jobcentres.

The YTS is intended to provide a transition between school and work by giving young people work experience and a certain amount of training both on and off the job. They also have the opportunity to get certain vocational qualifications. At the end of the training period they get a certificate which records the skills and qualifications they have obtained and an assessment of their abilities. They get a certificate even if they leave the scheme early to take up a job they are offered.

On the scheme they may be regarded either as trainees or employees. Trainees normally get a tax-free training allowance which in 1988 is a rather meagre £28.50 a week in the first year and £35 a week from then on. They do not have to pay any National Insurance contributions as they are credited with them. But they do not get any employment rights other than general protection regarding discrimination and health and safety at work, and they can ask to have time off to go to interviews for jobs. If they are ill for more than three weeks they may lose their allowance and their place on the scheme (though they may be able to get another when they are well again).

People regarded as employees get a contract of employment and normal employment rights, and are paid a wage which should be in line with other employees in the firm. If the wage is high enough for tax and National Insurance to be due, these will be deducted from what they get.

It is unlikely that people on the Youth Training Scheme will be able to claim any social security benefits, and anyone who leaves the scheme before completion (or refuses a place on it without good reason) is likely to have their income support reduced for the next 13 weeks.

Part-time courses

For any young person without a job, taking further training or education is obviously a sensible use of time. It will be worth their enquiring about courses available at a local Further Education College, Technical College or Sixth Form College. Between them, these colleges offer a wide range of vocational courses as well as the chance to get more GCSEs and A levels. The local education authority will normally pay the college's fees for anyone under 19 as long as they agree that the course is suitable. Students who follow a full-time course (which means more than 21 hours a week of tuition time, not counting private study or homework) will lose their entitlement to income support (though there are exceptions for disabled students), but they may be able to get a small grant (see next page). They can, however, follow part-time courses for up to 21 hours a week and still get income support as long as both following the course does not prevent them from taking a job (because, for example, all the classes are in the evening and they only study in the evenings); otherwise they must be prepared to give up their studies at any time if a suitable job comes up; and they must have been getting income support, unemployment benefit or sickness benefit for the 13 weeks before the course starts; or they must have been getting one of these benefits for at least 13 of the last 26 weeks and been in a full-time job for the rest; or they must have been on a Youth Training Scheme.

This last point means that, except in special circumstances, young people cannot go straight from school on to 21 hours of further education and get income support.

Full-time students

Full-time students are eligible to receive grants, but you may well find that you are still in part supporting your son or daughter as you may be expected to contribute towards their upkeep. Many students will find that they can claim social security benefits to supplement their income.

Student grants

Grants for full-time students fall into two main categories. There are *mandatory* awards for people on 'designated' courses: a university or CNAA degree, Diploma of Higher Education, BTEC Higher Diploma, teacher training, university certificate or diploma courses lasting at least three years, and certain other courses.

There are also *discretionary* awards for full-time students on lower-level courses, such as at technical colleges and further education colleges. These grants are quite small and it is entirely up to the local education authority whether they give your child one. They may reserve them for the few people they think are the most deserving cases.

In both cases, unless your child is regarded as an 'independent' student (which means being over 25 or having supported him- or herself for the previous three years) your income will be taken into account in working out how much is given. You can get further information on these maintenance grants from your local education authority – see *Grants to Students* published by the Department of Education and Science each year.

Grants for Higher Education

To qualify for a mandatory grant, a person must normally have lived in the UK for the previous three years, and must not have already attended certain similar courses. You apply to the local education authority for the area in which you live, preferably well before the course starts. The grant falls into two parts. The first part covers all the course fees (which the education authority pays to the college direct). This is paid on behalf of everyone who qualifies. Then most students also get a maintenance grant to live on during term time and the Christmas and Easter vacations. The amount paid for this part of the grant is a standard figure, but it is reduced on a sliding scale if the student's or parents' income is high, and the parents are expected to make up the shortfall. So students whose parents are very well off may receive nothing for maintenance, it being expected that their parents will give them the amount of the maintenance grant each term.

The maximum amount of maintenance grant depends on where the student lives while at college. If he or she is provided with free board and lodging by the college the maximum in the 1988–89 academic year is £895, while if they live at home it is £1,630. In other circumstances – living in a college hall of residence or a flat or lodgings – the maximum is £2,425 in London and £2,050 elsewhere. Students who are married, have children, are over 26 or are disabled may get higher amounts. Students may also get more if their college terms are longer than normal, if they are required to study abroad or away from their normal college, or if they need special equipment for certain subjects.

Having established the maximum maintenance grant your child is entitled to, the process of reduction begins. First, if the student's own income from certain other sources (investments, for example) in the academic year is more than a certain amount (£525 in 1988–89), the amount of grant is reduced by the excess. For example, if he or she had £600 income from these other sources, the grant would be reduced by £75. 'Income' here means income from most sources, but the following are ignored:

- the student's earnings from work done either in holidays or term time
- the first £2,150 of any scholarship or payment from an employer
- payments from the student's parents under a deed of covenant
- child benefit, guardian's allowance, income support, housing benefit, attendance allowance and mobility allowance and supplement.

Unless the student is regarded as 'independent' (which means being over 25 or having supported him- or herself for the previous three years), or his or her parents are dead or cannot be found, the parents' income will be taken into account and may reduce the amount of grant paid. If the student is married and the parents cannot be asked to make a contribution to the grant, the student's husband or wife may be expected to make a contribution, worked out in a similar way to a parental contribution but on a different scale.

The parental contribution

The income of both parents is counted in assessing the amount you should contribute, unless you are separated. The figure used is your income for tax purposes in the tax year before the academic year (for instance the 1987–88 tax year for the 1988–89 academic year) before any personal allowances are deducted. To this is added any money paid out of a trust fund for the education or maintenance of anyone dependent on you. From this total is subtracted the gross amount of interest you paid which qualifies for tax relief (e.g. on a mortgage), up to

£1,285 for each adult dependent on you, and half the amount paid in premiums on a qualifying life insurance policy taken out before 13 March 1984. The cost of employing help in the home and extra allowances for parents who are themselves students or who live abroad may also be deducted in some circumstances. This leaves what is called the parents' 'residual income'.

The amount of parental contribution depends on the amount of this residual income and on when the student started his or her course of higher education. Parents of students starting their course in autumn 1988 will have their contribution assessed on a more generous new scale, to make up for the ending of tax relief on covenanted contributions, and the grant from the LEA will be increased accordingly (i.e. by 25 per cent). Parents of students already embarked on their course will have their contribution assessed on the old scale, whether or not they have covenanted their contribution to the student. So, in 1988–89:

If the residual income is:	Parent's contribution is:	
	Old scale	*New scale*
under £9,900	nil	nil
£9,900 to £12,600	£50 plus £1 for each £7 over £9,900	£37 plus £1 for each £9.33 over £9,900
£12,601 to £18,400	£435 plus £1 for each £5 over £12,600	£326 plus £1 for each £6.67 over £12,600
From £18,401	£1,515 plus £1 for each £4 over £18,400	£1,136 plus £1 for each £5.33 over £18,400

(up to a maximum of £4,900)

Your contribution is then reduced by £260 for each other child who gets a grant and by £100 for each other dependent child not on a grant.

If you have more than one child on a grant, the parental contribution is divided between them – it does not have to be paid for each child. Your total contribution will not be more than £4,900, however many student children you have.

Social security benefits

Students who have worked and paid National Insurance contributions before starting their courses can claim unemployment benefit during the long summer vacations. To qualify they must meet all the normal conditions (see p.118). Students used to be able to claim benefit during the Christmas and Easter vacations if they met an extra condition, but they are no longer allowed to do so. They cannot claim during term time as they are not regarded as being available for work.

For the same reason, most students will not be able to claim income support during term time, but there are four exceptions:
- single parents
- the disabled and handicapped, who find it difficult to obtain work within a reasonable time
- those who live with someone they are not married to and who is not a student, and who has a child who is dependent on the student
- those who live with someone they are not married to and who is not a student, and who has been unable to work for eight weeks or more through illness or injury.

Students in these circumstances do not have to be available for work to get income support during term time or the Christmas and Easter vacations. The grant will be counted in their income when working out how much benefit they are entitled to in these periods.

Other students can only claim income support during the long summer vacation. Any grant and parental contribution they get will be ignored in working out how much benefit they are entitled to, but if parents give them extra money over the year by deed of covenant (see below) this extra will count as income.

Many students living away from home will also find that they are eligible for housing benefit. Information about these and other benefits you may be able to claim is given in DHSS leaflet FB.23 *Going to College or University? – A Pocket Guide to Social Security*.

Covenants for students

Before the 1988 Budget it was possible for parents to reduce the cost of their parental contributions by making the payments under a deed of covenant. The effect was that the parent got tax relief on the amount paid over, and the student would not have to pay tax on it if his or her income, including the covenanted payments, came to less than his or her personal tax allowances.

Tax relief will continue to apply to existing covenants which were made before 15 March 1988 and sent to a tax inspector by 30 June 1988. But it is no longer possible to get tax relief on any other new covenants.

The money a parent pays by deed of covenant will not normally affect the amount of grant the student gets. But if the student counts as 'independent', or if the covenant payments are from anyone else, they will count as the student's income and if this is more than a certain limit the grant will be reduced pound for pound (see p.131). 'Anyone else' includes a separated parent who is not obliged to make a parental contribution.

10 Leaving money to children

Why you should make a will

There are several reasons why everyone should have a will, but particularly anyone with children. First, it is the only way of making sure that your possessions go to the people you want to have them. Second, it is your opportunity to say who you want to look after your children should anything happen to you and your partner. Third, provided the will is properly drawn up, it makes everything easier for your relatives to sort things out after your death. Fourth, a bit of planning can mean that a lot less tax is payable by your heirs on the value of what you leave – meaning more money for them.

Drawing up a will is fairly straightforward, and there are a number of books available which can tell you exactly how to do it. Alternatively, you may feel it is worthwhile discussing your wishes with a solicitor, who will then draft the will for you. A solicitor should also be able to advise you on whether it would be worth your considering setting up a trust and whether there are any particular aspects of inheritance tax for you to watch out for. It is worth going to a solicitor as they do not usually charge much more than £30 or so for drawing up a will unless your circumstances are complicated, and it is very important that the will is drawn up properly; otherwise it will be declared void and the position will be the same as if you had not left one. There are important rules about how a will is set out, signed and witnessed.

It is in your and your children's interest to make sure that your husband, wife or partner also makes a will. It is obviously sensible if you sort them out together to make sure that each of you is happy with your partner's wishes, but there is no obligation on either of you to tell the other that you have made a will or what it says. If you are married and your permanent home is in England or Wales, it is important that your will was made since your marriage; if it was made before it may no longer be valid.

Having made your will, make sure that your partner knows where it is kept. It is sensible if you deposit a copy with your solicitor or bank. It is also very helpful to make a list of life insurance policies you have, a list of where documents are kept and a list of the organizations which would need to be contacted on your death, and leave copies of these with your wills.

Who inherits if you don't make a will

If you die without leaving a will, the rules about who inherits what depend on what are called the rules of intestacy, which are different in different parts of the United Kingdom.

In England and Wales everything depends on whether you are married at the time of death. If you are, your spouse gets all your personal belongings (such as a car, furniture, clothing). Then if you have no children, your spouse gets the next £85,000 of your estate plus half the rest. The remainder goes to your parents or, if they are dead, to your brothers and sisters. If you also have no surviving brothers or sisters everything goes to your spouse. If you do have children, your spouse gets only the next £40,000 and the rest is split in two. One half is divided immediately among the children. Your spouse gets a 'life interest' in the other half, meaning that he or she has the right to use it as long as he or she lives but on his or her death it will pass to your children.

If you are not married at the time of death, your possessions are divided equally amongst your nearest group of relatives in the following order: children (including adopted children, step-children and illegitimate children), parents, full brothers and sisters, half-brothers and sisters, grandparents, uncles and aunts, half-brothers or half-sisters of parents. For example, if you have no surviving children or parents but a brother, your brother will get everything and people further down the list nothing. If someone who would have inherited has died but their children are living, their share will be divided amongst those children. If there are no relatives entitled to inherit, everything passes to the Crown. This system applies if you have been living with someone you are not married to, as a common-law husband or wife inherits nothing from their partner under English law.

Much the same applies in Northern Ireland, but in Scotland the rules are quite different. If your permanent home is in Scotland and you die without leaving a will, your husband or wife (and normally a common-law husband or wife) will inherit your home, unless it is worth more than £50,000 in which case they will inherit just £50,000. They will also get the first £10,000 worth of its contents. If there are no surviving children, your spouse also gets the next £25,000 plus half what is left (the remaining half goes to the nearest relatives). If there are children, your spouse gets the next £15,000 plus one third of what is left (the remaining two thirds are split between the children).

What you can leave

If you are married, things which you own jointly will normally become your husband's or wife's sole property when you die. But marriage does not mean that you own everything jointly with your husband or wife. In general, things which you owned before the marriage or which you inherited, were given, won or bought with your own money are yours to leave to whoever you like in your will.

But there are some exceptions to this. An important one in England and Wales concerns a jointly owned home. Legally, there are two types of joint ownership, the more common one being called joint tenancy. With this, if one of you dies, your share automatically passes to the other, even if the will says something else. You cannot leave your share to anyone other than the joint owner. The other type of tenancy is called tenancy-in-common, under which you own your shares in the home independently and can each leave your share to whoever you like in your will (though the joint owner could dispute this after your death). If you do not know which type of joint ownership you have you can find out from the deeds of the home or ask your solicitor.

If your permanent home is in Scotland, there are some restrictions on who you can leave things to in your will. If you are married or live with someone as man and wife, you must leave your partner at least one third of your estate (one half if you have no children). If you have children you must leave them at least one third of your estate (one half if you have no husband or wife or common-law husband or wife).

Inheritance tax and its consequences

Inheritance tax replaced capital transfer tax in March 1986. There are two main differences. Firstly, while both taxes apply to the value of your estate when you die, capital transfer tax was also payable if you made gifts of more than a certain value in any period of ten years at any point in your life. As far as lifetime gifts to people are concerned, inheritance tax applies only to things you give away in the last seven years of your life. Secondly, you could get round capital transfer tax to a large extent by putting things into a trust but still continue to use them and even get them back eventually if you wanted to.

LEAVING MONEY TO CHILDREN

Trusts can still enable you to keep some control over things you give away, but if you continue to get any benefit from them you will not be regarded as having given them away for inheritance tax purposes. They will continue to be treated as part of your estate, so there will be no tax saving if, for example, you live in a home you have put into a trust or get any benefit from the income from investments you have transferred to one of your children.

Of course, your estate may not be valuable enough for much, if any, tax to be payable. In 1988–89 the threshold is £110,000, and it is likely to increase in line with inflation each year. There is no tax to be paid if your estate (plus the value of certain things you gave away in the last seven years of your life) is worth less than this threshold. If it is more, the basic rule is that tax is charged on the excess at a single rate of 40%.

Not everything that you leave when you die or give away in the last seven years of your life is subject to inheritance tax. The following gifts are totally ignored, whenever you make them:

- gifts to a husband or wife (even if you are separated)
- gifts to charities, political parties, universities, public museums, art galleries and certain national institutions like the National Trust
- approved gifts of heritage property (e.g. land, buildings and works of art of outstanding national, historic or artistic interest) to non-profit-making bodies.

There are also special rules for businesses, farms, farmland and woodland which mean that less than the normal amount of tax will be payable. Gifts to your children are not exempt, apart from providing for their maintenance, education and upbringing.

There are two things which follow from these exemptions. The first is that because all gifts between husband and wife are exempt from inheritance tax, you and your spouse can give things to each other at any time. So if you each leave everything you own to the other in your wills, there will be no tax to pay on the first death. But the problem with this is that, on the second death, the total value of everything may be considerable and a large chunk may go in tax. You can get round this by arranging a joint life insurance policy which pays out enough on the second death to cover all or part of the probable tax bill. But it may be better for each of you to leave part of your estate to your spouse and part to your children. If the value of the things left to the children is no more than the current threshold for tax, there will still be no tax on the first death, and there should be a lot less on the second – so the children will get more in the end. But you should each make sure that your spouse will have enough to live on with what you are leaving them.

If one of you is worth very much more than the other (so that one has very little to leave to the children) the exemption on gifts between husband and wife means that you can transfer things between you to make the situation more even. You only need to transfer enough for the less-well-off spouse to have enough to leave to the children if he or she dies first. He or she can then leave everything they now own to the children, while the better-off spouse leaves some of their estate to the children and some to the less-well-off spouse.

The second point to notice about the exemptions is that you can reduce the value of your estate (and thus the tax payable) at any time by giving or leaving things to charities and various other bodies.

When you die, inheritance tax will be based on the total value of your estate (including your share of things owned jointly). This comprises the following, unless they count as exempt gifts (e.g. to your spouse or a charity):
- homes and land you own
- your car, furniture and other possessions
- any businesses you own
- your savings and investments (except money you have used to buy life annuities)

LEAVING MONEY TO CHILDREN

- the amount paid out by certain life insurance policies (see below)
- any money you are owed, and any interest you have in property or a trust or settlement
- the value of any gifts you have made in the last seven years of your life, except the exempt gifts listed below. The value used is the value at the time you made the gift (but if it has since gone down, the value at the time of death can be used).

Any money you own when you die is subtracted from your estate, and the costs of your funeral can also be paid out of your estate. If what is left is more than the current threshold for inheritance tax, tax is charged on the excess (though if you made any taxable gifts in the last seven years of your life, the way the tax is worked out is more complicated than this).

If you have any life insurance policies on your life, the amount each pays out on your death will count as part of your estate unless the policy is 'written in trust' for someone (see below). In the latter case, the money is paid direct to the person named in the policy and does not form part of your estate. Much the same applies to death benefits from pension schemes and personal pension plans: the money will not form part of your estate if, as is usual, the trustees have discretion about who it is paid to (they normally follow your wishes).

In your will you normally leave specific things or specific amounts of money to people you name and, because you do not know exactly how much your estate will be worth at the time you die, you also say who is to receive the rest (called the residue). Unless your will says otherwise, all the inheritance tax on what you leave will be payable out of the residue. But you can stipulate that the recipient of a particular item or amount of money pays any tax due on what they get.

Lifetime gifts

As stated above, inheritance tax is based not only on the value of what you leave when you die but also on the value of gifts you have made in the previous seven years. But in addition to the exemptions listed on the previous page, certain other types of gift which you make in your lifetime are ignored for inheritance tax. These are:

- wedding presents up to £5,000 if you are a parent, £2,500 if you are a grandparent or great-grandparent, otherwise £1,000
- gifts to help support members of your family – your husband or wife, a former spouse, a child under 18 or in full-time education, a dependent relative
- transfers to a former husband or wife, made as part of the divorce settlement
- gifts to your mother or mother-in-law if she is widowed, separated or divorced
- regular gifts of money made out of your income (not out of your capital) which do not affect your standard of living
- one-off gifts to as many people as you like, as long as what you give each person in each tax year is not worth more than £250.

In addition to all these, another £3,000 worth of gifts in any tax year will be ignored for inheritance tax. And if you do not use all the year's £3,000 allowance, you can use what remains in the following year (but not later). All the above allowances apply individually to a husband and wife.

Most other gifts you make are called Potentially Exempt Transfers (PETs). When you die, it is only the PETs which you have made in the last seven years which are included in your estate for tax purposes – earlier gifts are ignored. And with these tax may not be levied at full rate as any tax payable on things you gave away between three and seven years before your death is scaled down.

All the above applies to lifetime gifts to individual people, to accumulation and maintenance trusts (see p.104) and to trusts set up for benefit of disabled people. There are more stringent rules for what are called chargeable transfers – these are gifts involving companies and gifts that are made to discretionary trusts. If the value of the chargeable transfers you make in any seven year period exceeds the current threshold for inheritance tax (£110,000 in 1988–89) tax will become due straight away. It will be charged at 20%, but if you die within seven years extra tax may be payable.

The moral of all this is twofold. First, you do not have to worry about most modest gifts that you make – they will not mean any inheritance tax to pay on your death and, if you live for seven more years, will reduce the eventual tax bill. Second, if the value of your estate is large and will mean a sizable tax bill for your children and other heirs on your death, you can reduce the bill they will face by making gifts which fall into the exempt categories in your lifetime.

There are a few more specific tips which follow from the points above. The first is that one way of passing your money on to your children is to make regular payments into investments in their names. Again, as long as the payments came within the exemptions in the list above, the amount you paid would not be counted in your estate for inheritance tax purposes even if you were to die within seven years, and the investments would belong to your children. The only problem would be that the income from the investments would be taxed as if it was yours, not your children's (unless it was under £5 in the tax year). The result would normally be that income tax was payable on the income, whereas if it was treated as your child's it could probably escape tax. One way round this is to go for investments where all or most of the return is capital gain rather than income. Another way is to take out a life insurance policy which involves investment (an endowment policy) on your life which is written in trust for the child. Your payments into the policy can still count as regular payments made out of your income. If you were to die during the term of the policy, the sum insured would be paid direct to the child free of all tax and without having to wait for probate to be granted. If you outlived the policy, the child would get its final value on the maturity date, again free of all tax.

If you want to give things away in your lifetime, it is generally better to choose things which will grow in value and to hang on to things which produce an income. The things you have given away will then increase in value outside your estate, while the things you retain will provide you with an income in later life but not swell the value of your estate. But make sure that you do not give away assets which you and your partner will need to provide income in later life. You may need to check up on your pension provision and the death benefits your pension schemes provide.

A further consideration is that, as inheritance tax becomes payable on your death, you can take out life insurance to cover it. There are a number of circumstances in which this is worth considering. One case is if it looks as though things which you would like your heirs to inherit would have to be sold on your death to pay the tax. Another is if the tax on your estate is to be paid out of the residue but you cannot tell if the residue will be sufficient to cover it. Generally a whole life policy (which pays out whenever you die) will be most appropriate to cover all or some of the tax on things you leave when you die, though term insurance (which pays out if you die within the term of the policy) is cheaper. Also the younger you are and the better your health, the less insurance will cost. The policy should be written in trust to the person who will have to pay the tax, so that the money from it will not swell the size of your estate still further.

A similar consideration follows for people with valuable possessions and estates. If you have a very valuable asset such as a second home which you want to transfer in your lifetime, it is worth remembering that inheritance tax is only payable on gifts to people and certain trusts if you die within seven years. If you survive that period no inheritance tax will be payable, even if the property was worth millions (though watch out for capital gains tax – see next page). So it is worth arranging extra life insurance, such as a seven-year life insurance policy which would roughly meet the extra tax which would be due if you were to die within seven years of the gift. Most life insurance companies offer such policies. There are other types of life insurance which are appropriate in other circumstances – a suitable broker should be able to advise you.

Putting inheritance tax in context

Two important points should over-ride all the considerations above. The first is that you won't have to pay the tax, other people will. This is not as selfish as it may seem: the people who receive your gifts will be better off than they were, even after the tax has been paid. You might have given them nothing! (However, you will probably want your children to benefit as much as possible.) The second is that no one can foretell the future. Not only do you not know whether you are going to die within the next seven years, but you also do not know how the tax rules will be changed. So, while you will certainly make wiser decisions if you know what the basic rules are, you should certainly not deprive yourself or your partner of future capital or income that you might need, nor should you think that saving tax is the most important consideration in deciding when to give what to whom. For example, you could consider selling things you no longer need rather than giving them away, and then investing the money for your retirement and old age.

Capital Gains Tax on gifts

It is not often realized that capital gains tax (CGT) can arise if you give away valuable things to your children at any time in your life. The tax is normally thought of as a tax on the profit you make when you sell something, but it can also apply if something you give away is worth more than it was when you acquired it. For example, if you give away something which is worth £30,000 which was only worth £10,000 when you acquired it, there may be CGT to pay on part of the 'gain' of £20,000. But the tax now applies only to the increase in value

since April 1982, however long you have owned it. And certain gifts are exempt from CGT:
- gifts of money
- gifts between husband and wife
- your own home (unless you have run a business in part of it or let part of it out) or, if you have more than one home, the one you have nominated as your main one for capital gains tax purposes (whether or not this is the one you have lived in most of the time)
- cars, things worth less than £3,000, and things with an expected life of less than 50 years
- the first £125,000 of the increase in value of a business, if you give it away after age 60 and have owned it for more than ten years (there is further relief on gains up to £500,000)
- certain investments – National Savings Certificates, Yearly Plan, Premium Bonds and Save As You Earn; British Government stocks; proceeds from life insurance policies
- anything you leave to other people on your death

The increase in value since April 1982 of most other things that you sell or give away in the tax year is added up and if it comes to more than the current threshold for CGT (£5,000 in 1988–89) the excess will be added to your income and taxed at the same rates as income tax (it is actually rather more complicated than this, as allowances can be made for costs incurred in buying and selling and for inflation over the period you have owned it since 1982). This means you can avoid capital gains tax if you can make sure that the total increase in value since April 1982 of things you give away in any tax year is no more than the current threshold. It is therefore easier to avoid CGT on things like valuable pieces of furniture which you can give away in reasonable amounts each year than it is on things like a second home which you can only give away all at once.

If you are married, the yearly CGT threshold applies to the total both husband and wife give away; you do not each get a tax-free allowance. In this respect CGT is different from inheritance tax, though it is planned that from April 1990 husband

and wife will each have their own threshold. Remember, too, that while inheritance tax is based on the value of things at the time you give them away, CGT is based only on the amount they have increased in value since you acquired them or since April 1982, whichever was later.

Another point about CGT is that if both the person making the gift and the person getting it agree, the 'gain' can be held over until the recipient eventually disposes of it. The gift will then be ignored when it is made, but when the recipient eventually gets rid of it the 'gain' will be taken to be the amount the item has increased in value since the time when the *giver* acquired it.

What your will should say

Having considered the tax effects of gifts that you make and of the estate you leave when you die, you are now in a position to decide what you should leave in your will and to whom, and what you might consider giving away in your lifetime to provide for other people or to reduce the possible inheritance tax liability.

But first, your will should say that you revoke all previous wills you have made and it should name your executors. These are the people who will take over your possessions temporarily when you die, pay any debts and any tax due, apply for probate (official recognition that the will is valid) and see that your wishes in the will are carried out. You should, of course, ask these people if they are willing to act as your executors before naming them in your will – it can be quite a tiresome job. You can have several executors, and you should name alternatives in case any dies before you. It is sensible if your husband or wife is one, and also a child of yours. Solicitors and banks will also act as executors, but they will have to be paid out of your estate.

If you have children, use your will to name guardians for them in case both you and your husband or wife die before they are 18. Again, you should make sure that the people you name are willing to take on the job. You will also need to consider how your children would be provided for until they are 18. They cannot inherit from you directly: anything you leave them has by law to be held in trust for them until they are 18. It may therefore be sensible to appoint as trustees the same people as you have appointed to be their guardians. Unless your will says otherwise the trustees will be your executors and will have to sell any property you leave the children and invest the money. They can spend the income from this and up to half the capital on the children's maintenance and education (if necessary) and give each child his or her remaining share of the trust money on reaching 18.

Next, your will should say which of your possessions and how much of your money is to go to whom. You can, of course, leave everything to one person or one organization or any number of them. If you are leaving things to your husband or wife, it is sensible to include the condition that they outlive you by, say, 30 days and that if they do not the things are to go to someone else. If you did not do this and you died a few days before your spouse (as a result of the same accident, say), your estate would be added to your spouse's before being passed on according to your spouse's will, and only the first £110,000 (or whatever the current threshold was) of the total would be free of inheritance tax. But with the 30-day clause, your and your wife's estates would remain separate and £110,000 of each would be free of tax. The difference in the amount of tax payable could be £40,000 or more.

Unless you are leaving everything to one person or organization, your will should next say who is to receive the residue of your estate. As mentioned earlier, any inheritance tax due on what you leave in your will is normally payable out of the residue, unless you have said that any of your specific gifts are to bear their own tax.

In each case you should also name the person you would like to get something if your first choice dies before you. Alternatively, you can name a class of people rather than naming individuals – such as 'shared equally between all my surviving children'. If there is no survivor to receive a specific gift it is added to the residue. If there is no survivor to receive the residue, it is treated as if you had died without leaving a will (see p.136).

Your will can also say whether you want to donate any parts of your body for transplant or research, and whether you want your body to be buried or cremated. Finally, it must be properly signed and witnessed (it is very important that none of the witnesses stand to gain anything from the will).

Although all the main considerations in making a will are given above, it is generally sensible to discuss your requirements with a solicitor and get him or her to draw up the will. You can then feel reasonably confident that your wishes will be carried out without any problems arising. It is hoped that the information above will enable you to make better choices which will benefit your children after your death as well as during your life.

11 Further information

One of the best sources of information on family finance is likely to be your local reference library. Many stock a large number of reference books, leaflets and pamphlets, and library staff should be able to tell you where to find information they do not have themselves. Many reference libraries keep stocks of leaflets produced by Government departments and local councils, so a trip to the library may save you several visits to other offices.

For advice on many of the subjects covered in this book, a good place to make enquiries is your local Citizens Advice Bureau (CAB). They will be able to give you a lot of help with certain types of problem, all free of charge. If they cannot help directly, they will be able to tell you where to go for advice. You can make an appointment or just call in.

In some areas there are Money Advice Centres, where you can get free and unbiased help with your money problems. Your library or CAB should be able to tell you if there is one near you and where it is. But don't forget you can ask for advice and information from the offices of government and local council departments. For information about tax ask at your local tax or PAYE enquiry office, listed in the phone book under 'Inland Revenue – Taxes, H.M. Inspectors of.' You can get information about social security benefits by phoning Freephone DHSS or by calling at a local DHSS office. These are listed in the phone book under 'Health and Social Security, Dept of – Local Social Security Offices'. For information about housing and housing benefits you will normally need to ask at the housing department of your local council. In all cases it is worth ringing before you go to check up on opening and closing times and make sure the office is the correct one for your particular enquiry.

If you have a lot of money at your disposal there is likely to be a range of professional advisers who will be anxious to help you – bank managers, accountants, life insurance salesmen and brokers, investment advisers, and so on. While many of the services they can offer are excellent, it is worth remembering that they make their living by selling them. Always make sure you understand exactly what is involved in any scheme you are considering, satisfy yourself that you really need it and make sure you can afford it.

Money

Local Citizens Advice Bureau or Money Advice Centre

Accountant, bank manager, investment adviser, insurance broker, building society manager, solicitor, etc.

Further reading
The Guardian Money Guide, Margaret Dibben (Collins Willow, £4.95)
Making the Most of Your Money, Louise Botting and Vincent Duggleby (Orbis, £5)
The Money Book, Margaret Allen (Pan, £4.95)
Which? Book of Saving and Investing (Consumers' Association/Hodder & Stoughton, £10.95)
Which? Book of Tax (Consumers' Association/Hodder & Stoughton, £12.95)

Write Your Own Will, Keith Best (Elliott Right Way Books, £1.20)

Your home

Local Housing Aid Centre

Housing Department of your local council
SHAC (the London Housing Aid Centre), 189a Old Brompton Road, London SW5 0AR

Building Societies' Association, 3 Savile Row, London W1X 1AF

Further reading
Housing booklets, Department of the Environment (free from libraries and CAB)
Building Societies and House Purchase (The Building Societies Association, free)
Renting and Letting (Consumers' Association/Hodder & Stoughton, £5.95)
Rights Guide for Home Owners, Joe Tunnard & Clare Whately (SHAC, £2.50)
Which? Way to Buy, Sell and Move House (Consumers' Association/Hodder & Stoughton, £8.95)

State benefits

Local Social Security office or CAB

Child Poverty Action Group (CPAG), 1 Macklin Street, London WC2B 5NH

Further reading
Maternity Rights Handbook, Ruth Evans and Lyn Durward (Penguin, £4.95)

National Welfare Benefits Handbook, Ruth Cohen & Beth Lakhani (CPAG, £4)
Rights Guide to Non-Means-Tested Social Security Benefits, Roger Smith & Mark Rowland (CPAG, £4)
Social Security Benefit Rates (leaflet NI.196, free from Social Security offices)
Tolley's Social Security and State Benefits, Jim Matthewman (Tolley's, £13.95)
Which Benefit? (leaflet FB.2, free from Social Security offices)

Unemployment

Local Jobcentre or Careers Office

Unemployment Benefit Office (see under 'Employment, Dept of' in phone book)

Further reading
How to Survive Unemployment, Robert Nathan and Michel Syrett (Penguin, £2.95)
Supplementary Benefit for Unemployed People (leaflets SB.9 and SB.21, free from Social Security offices)
Unemployed? Help You Can Get (leaflet FB.9, free from Social Security offices)
Unemployment Benefit (leaflet NI.12, free from Social Security offices)
The Unemployment Handbook, Guy Dauncey (National Extension College, £2.90)

Separation and divorce

National Council for the Divorced and Separated, 13 High Street, Little Shelford, Cambridge CB2 5ES

Families Need Fathers, 37 Carden Road, London SE15

Further reading
Divorce and Your Money, William Harper (Unwin, £1.95)
Divorce: Legal Procedures and Financial Facts (Consumers' Association/Hodder & Stoughton, £6.95)
How to Conduct Your Own Divorce, Gil Friedman (Futura, £2.95)
Undefended Divorce (free from County Courts)
A Woman's Place, Sue Witherspoon (SHAC, £2.50)

Widowhood

Cruse (the national organization for the widowed and their children), Cruse House, 126 Sheen Road, Richmond, Surrey TW19 1UR

National Association of Widows, Chell Road, Stafford ST16 2QA

Further reading
Survival Guide for Widows, June Hemer & Ann Stanyer (Age Concern, £3.50)
What to Do When Someone Dies (Consumers' Association/Hodder & Stoughton, £6.95)
Wills and Probate (Consumers' Association/Hodder & Stoughton, £6.95)

One-parent families

Gingerbread (Association for One-Parent Families), 35 Wellington Street, London WC2E 7BN

National Council for One-Parent Families, 255 Kentish Town Road, London NW5 2LX

Further reading
Bringing up Children? (leaflet FB.27, free from Social Security offices)

One-Parent Families – Help with Housing, Department of the Environment (free from CAB and libraries)

Unmarried couples

Further reading
The Cohabitation Handbook, Anne Bottomley et al. (Pluto Press, £5.50)
Going it Alone: A Guide for Unmarried Women, Anne McNicholas (SHAC, £2.50)
Living Together, Clare Dyer & Marcel Berlins (Hamlyn, £1.50)

Women's interests

Rights for Women, 374 Gray's Inn Road, London WC1X 8BB

National Women's Aid Federation, 374 Gray's Inn Road, London WC1X 8BB

Further reading
Money Guide for Women, Nigel Smith & Jill Greatorex (Coronet Books, £3.50)
Women's Rights, Anna Coote & Tess Gill (Penguin, £3.95)
The Working Woman's Guide, Liz Hodgkinson (Thorsons, £4.95)

The Disabled

The Disability Alliance, 25 Denmark Street, London WC2H 8NJ

The Spastics Society, 12 Park Crescent, London W1N 4EQ

Further reading
Benefits for Kids (from the Spastics Society, unpriced but donation appreciated)

Directory for Disabled People, Ann Darnbrough and Derek Kinrade (Woodhead-Faulkner, £11.50)
Disability Rights Handbook, ed. Sally Robertson (Disability Alliance, £2.60)
Help for Handicapped People (leaflet HB.1, free from Social Security offices)

Children

Child Poverty Action Group (CPAG), 1 Macklin Street, London WC2B 5NH

British Agencies for Adopting and Fostering (BAAF), 11 Southwark Street, London SE11 1RQ

Further reading
Bringing up Children? (leaflet FB.27, free from Social Security offices)
Children, Parents and the Law (Consumers' Association/Hodder & Stoughton, £5.95)
Fostering in the Eighties, Jane Rowe (BAAF, £2)
Income Tax and School Leavers (leaflet IR.33, free from tax offices)
Leaving School? (leaflet FB.20, free from Social Security offices)
The Step-Parents' Handbook, Elizabeth Hodder (Sphere, £2.95)
Yours by Choice: A Guide for Adoptive Parents, Jane Rowe (Routledge, £3.95)

Education

Education Department of your local council

Independent Schools Information Service (ISIS), 56 Buckingham Gate, London SW1E 6AG

National Union of Students (NUS), 461 Holloway Road, London N7 6LZ

Further reading
Decisions at 13/14, Michael Smith & Veronica Matthew (CRAC, £2.50)
Decisions at 15/16, Michael Smith (CRAC, £2.20)
Going to College or University? – A Pocket Guide to Social Security (leaflet FB.23, free from Social Security offices)
Grants to Students, published yearly by the Department of Education and Science.
Local Education Authority Awards Survey, National Union of Students, £2
A Parent's Guide to Education (Consumers' Association/Hodder & Stoughton, £5.95)
The School-Leaver's Handbook, ed. Jacquie Hughes (Adamson Books, £3.95)
The NUS Welfare Manual, National Union of Students
The Student Book, ed. K. Boehm *et al*, (Papermac, £7.95)
Which School? ed. Julia Padbury (Truman & Knightly Educational Trust, £7.70)

Insurance

Association of British Insurers, Aldermary House, Queen Street, London EC4N 1TU

Further reading
How to Plan your Life Insurance, Christopher Gilchrist (Martin Books, £4.95)
Value-for-Money Insurance, British Insurance Brokers' Association (Flame Books, £2.95)

Index

ACAS 32–3
access to children 57
accident insurance 117
accumulation trusts 92, 142
additional personal tax allowance 71–2, 74–5
affiliation orders 72
annuities (school fee payment) 125
'attachment of earnings' orders 69
attendance allowance 115
au pairs 86–7

Baby, initial costs 11–12
bank accounts, children's 98
birth, time off work 29
British Government Stock ('gilts') 14–15
budgeting 19–24
budget loans (Social Fund) 52
building society accounts 13–14, 97–8

Capital gains tax 94, 106, 144, 145–7
capital transfer tax 138
child benefit 38
childminders 81
children's earnings 88–90
  National Insurance 93–4
  taxation of 90–3, 106
  see also savings, children's

child's special allowance 73
Class F Land Charges 56
community care grants 52
company shares 15–16
covenants 95, 134
credit cards 18–19
crisis loans 53
custody 57, 62

Day nurseries 80–81
dental treatment, free 28
disabled persons' trusts 142
discretionary grants 129
divorce 54–5
  children and 57–8, 62
  home and possessions 56, 62–4
  injunctions 55–6
  living arrangements 55
  maintenance 65–9
  money matters 58–60
  social security 60
  tax allowances 60–2
  wills 65

Education
  additional costs 120–22
  employer-paid 122
  fee planning 123–6
  LEA assistance 121–2
  see also further education
endowment life insurance 122, 143
executors of wills 147
Family credit 43–4

'family income benefit' term life insurance 109
family income supplement 44
further education 128–34

Gifts to children 94–5
Gingerbread 82
guardian's allowance 39
guardians 148

Health insurance 155–17
Home Responsibilities Protection 37
house purchase 16
housing benefit 40–43, 134

Illness, benefits during 27–8, 113–15
  see also income support
income support 44–51, 126–8, 133
Independent School Information Services (ISIS) 126
Independent Schools Yearbook 125
'independent' students 129, 131
Index-Linked National Savings Certificates 102
Index-Linked stock 102–3
inheritance tax 100, 112–3, 138–45, 148

INDEX

inheritance tax (cont)
  chargeable transfers 142–3
  estate inclusions 140–41
  exempt gifts 139, 142–3
  Potentially Exempt Transfers 142
  thresholds 139
  trusts and 106, 138–9
  see also capital gains tax
injunctions 55–6
Inner London Education Authority (ILEA) 121
insurance
  accident 117
  health 115–17
  life 107–13
  taxation and 140, 141, 143, 144, 145
  unemployment 119
intestacy 136–7, 149
invalidity benefit 28, 114, 115
investment 13–16, 112–13
  see also savings, children's

Joint accounts 59
joint house ownership 138
joint-life insurance 111

Land Charges, Class F 56
Legal Aid scheme 54–5
life insurance
  arranging 111–12

life assurance (cont)
  cover needed 109–10
  endowment 112, 143
  'family income benefit' term 109
  investment policies 112–13
  joint-life 111
  self-employed 112
  taxation and 140–5
  'term insurance' 108–9, 144
  unit-linked 112
  whole-life 112, 144
  'written in trust' 104, 112, 141, 144
lifetime gifts 142–4
loans 18–19
lone parents 70–75
lump sum maternity payments 28

Maintenance orders 57, 59–60, 65, 68–9
maintenance payments 65
  insufficient 69
  late payment 68–9
  legal enforcement 57, 59–60, 65, 68–9
  'old' and 'new' agreements 66
  tax allowances 61, 66–8
  see also affiliation orders
mandatory grants 129, 130–31
Manpower Services Commission 127
maternity
  allowance 26–7
  benefits, problems 32–3

maternity (cont)
  leave 31
  lump sum payments 28
  social fund payments 52
  statutory pay 26–9
medical treatment, free 28
mobility allowance 115
Money Advice Centres 150
mortgages 16–18, 56

Nannies 83–5
National Childminding Association 81
National Council for One-Parent Families 72
National Insurance
  childrens's income 93–4
  contributions 37, 113, 115, 118, 126, 127, 133
  employer, as 84–6
  Home Responsibilities Protection 37
National Savings 13-14
  Bonds Office 14
  children's 97–100
  Index-Linked 102
nursery facilities
  day nurseries 80–1
  employer-provided 78–9
  employing someone in the home 84–6
  nursery schools 79–80
  playgroups 81–2
  self-provided 82–3

nursery facilities (cont)
  nursery schools 79–80

One-parent benefit 60, 70–71

Part-time further education courses 128
paternity leave 29
pension entitlement 36–8
playgroups 81–2
pregnancy
  right to return to work 29–32
  time off work 29
  unfair dismissal 29–30
Pre-School Playgroups Association 82

Redundancy payments 118
'residual income' 132

Savings, children's 95–6
  bank accounts 98
  building societies 97–8
  inheritance tax 100, 106, 112, 113
  investments 99–106
  life insurance 104, 112
  National Savings 97–100, 102
  trusts 104–6
  where to save 96–7, 99
    see also children's earnings

SAYE building society accounts 14
scholarships from employers 122
school fees 123–6
school leavers, unemployed 126–7
self-employed life insurance 112
severe disablement 115
sickness benefit 27, 113–14, 115
Social Fund 51–3
statutory maternity pay 25–6
statutory sick pay 27, 113
students
  covenants for 134
  grants 129, 130–3
  social security 133–4
supplementary benefit 45, 46, 47, 51

Tax allowances
  additional personal 61, 71–2, 74–5
  children's work 90–93
  divorce and 60–62
  life insurance 112
  married man's 34–5, 60–61
  separate taxation 36
  single person 34
  student covenants 134
  transference 35–6
  wife's 35–6, 60–61
taxation
  capital gains 138, 144, 145–7
  children's work 90–3, 106

taxation (cont)
  inheritance 100, 106, 112–13, 138–45, 148
  insurance 116, 112–13, 140–45
  scholarships 122
  trusts 92, 106, 138–9
trustees (children's) 148
trusts 92, 138–9, 142

Unemployment benefit 118–19, 133
unemployment insurance 119
unit-linked life insurance 112
unit trusts 15
unmarried couples 74–6

Wards of Court 57
widower's benefits 73
widow's benefits 73–4
wills
  bequests 137–8
  form and wording 147–9
  guardians, trustees 148
  intestacy 136–7, 149
  lifetime gifts 142–4
  making 135–6
  separations and 65
Women's Aid refuges 57
women, working, benefits for 29

Yearly Plan (National Savings) 14
Youth Training Scheme 46, 126–8